Two Roads
through
Narnia

FOR JOEL

Kathy Bledsoe

Jenn Wright

Two Roads
through
Narnia

Literary Analysis & Spiritual Commentary

Greg Wright, Editor
with Kathy Bledsoe, George Rosok & Jenn Wright

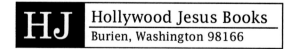
HJ Hollywood Jesus Books
Burien, Washington 98166

For Donna West
who urged us further up and further in

Contents

Spirituality, Art and Narnia
The Middle Path and Roads Less Traveled

Introduction by Greg Wright

One of the better television advertising campaigns of the Twentieth Century was conducted by the manufacturer of Reese's Peanut Butter Cups. The general scenario was the following:

One person is absorbed in eating a chocolate bar; another person, on a collision course with the first, is equally absorbed in a jar of peanut butter. The inevitable happens, and the chocolate bar winds up embedded in the jar of peanut butter. "You've got peanut butter on my chocolate!" complains the first person. "You've got chocolate in my peanut butter!" is the rejoinder. The two then taste the unexpected combination of peanut butter and milk chocolate and discover—to their mutual delight—that the accident was gastronomically fortuitous.

The genius of the ads—and the genius of the Reese's Peanut Butter Cup, too—is that they didn't try to sell the simple blending of the two tastes together. A Reese's works because the chocolate remains quite distinctly separate from the peanut butter. But the two together? Wow! Better than each by itself, because the tastes are distinct yet complementary. In the right proportion, the mix is cheap culinary heaven.

The Reese's Peanut Butter Cup, oddly enough, serves as an excellent metaphor for the effectiveness of *The Chronicles of Narnia*. The stories themselves, of course, cry out for commentary that limns their spiritual significance; and

1

C. S. Lewis, naturally, made no bones about the fact that such illumination was an intended end product of his fantasy.

But the spiritual aspect of the *Chronicles* is not the only flavor to be found therein, any more than peanut butter is the only flavor to be found in a Reese's Peanut Butter Cup. In fact, in the same way that peanut butter is the heart of a Reese's, wrapped carefully in a shroud of milk chocolate, the spirituality of the *Chronicles*—the heart that beats at its core—is carefully and deliberately packaged as literature. And just as the full flavor of a Reese's can't come alive without high-quality, carefully-formulated milk chocolate, the spiritual symbolism of Narnia can't be liberated without the *Chronicles*' first function as effective literature.

This is not to say the Christian spirituality embedded in the *Chronicles* is empty without the shell of Lewis' fantasy. Not at all. Peanut butter is still peanut butter, after all, and all the Reese's Peanut Butter Cups in the world, in all their now-varied flavors, cannot ever eliminate the appetite for pure, unadulterated peanut butter. Likewise, history has shown the human appetite for pure milk chocolate has continued unabated. But there's no denying that the unique Peanut Butter Cup taste has its own special appeal.

So let me be clearer. The Christian story—the Gospel itself, which Scripture declares to be "the power of God for the salvation of everyone who believes"[†]—is still the Christian story, and all the blockbuster fantasies in the world, whether *The Chronicles of Narnia* or *The Lord of the Rings*, cannot ever eliminate the human appetite for that which truly has the power to save. Likewise, the last fifty years have demonstrated that such spiritual literary fare has done little to quell the human taste for more "traditional" works of "pure" literature.

[†] Romans 1:16.

Introduction

Two Sides in the Debate

We should also be clear that, in the debate that continues to rage over the litero-spiritual Peanut Butter Cups that Narnia, Middle-earth and their cousins have spawned, there are two sets of gatekeepers who have vested interests in keeping chocolate out of the peanut butter jar, and peanut butter off the chocolate bars.

On the side of the chocolate bar are the academicians who still manage to dismiss such latter day epic myths as *The Chronicles of Narnia* and *The Lord of the Rings* as escapist fantasy, simple-minded romance or weak-minded Christian tripe. (I have to admit that, were I forced to choose between the two camps, this is the side on which I would fall. As we shall see, no such side-choosing is necessary.)

On the other side, the side of the peanut butter, are gleefully triumphant (if slightly paranoid) evangelical ministers of various denominations who champion Lewis and Tolkien (but particularly Lewis) as proof that literary endeavors of all other sorts are second rate at best and wholly irrelevant at worst.

Though both sides of this debate are misguided, Middle-earth and Narnia—because of the unique differences and stylistic leanings of their creators—do provide the perfect litmus test for discovering toward which side of the debate any given critic leans. Of *The Chronicles of Narnia*, academic purists will cry, "Ah! But you've got far too much sappy spirituality on my literature!" Of *The Lord of the Rings*, evangelical ministers (like me) often object, "Wait! There's far too much literature overwhelming my spirituality!"

So far in this discussion, of course, I've painted almost everyone (including myself) with very broad strokes of a very messy and over-generalized brush. And since neither of those sets of gatekeepers are my real subject, I will make no attempt to defend my generalizations with citations from specific critics who prove my point. Why? Because there's a third approach about which I'm more concerned.

A Third Poor Option

This third approach attempts to pretend that Reese's Peanut Butter Cups (and their analogs) exist in a universe of their own. This approach admirably attempts to walk a middle path while wearing blinders. Blinders, of course, are very useful if all you're doing is pulling the wagon and someone else is holding the reins. But if you're responsible for both the pulling and the guidance (and particularly if guidance is your primary job), blinders are a hazard both to you and everything that you guide.

The problem is that this approach appreciates a Peanut Butter Cup only for its effect. Such an appreciation is deficient not only because it ignores the fact that a Reese's was designed with both milk chocolate and peanut butter in mind, but also because it can only explain why a Reese's is wonderful in self-referential terms. Listening to this brand of enthusiast, we might get the impression that the real point of a Reese's is simply the mixing of peanut butter with chocolate, and that any old type of either ingredient would do.

But great spiritual literature isn't made of garden-variety books filled with grade-B theology. Great spiritual literature is written by excellent writers of great faith.

So to blindly champion "spiritual art"—or so-called Christian books, Christian music and Christian movies, to be blunt—simply because it's easily identifiable as "Christian" does both art and Christianity a great disservice. The *Left Behind* series, while enormously entertaining, is, to be brutally honest, neither great writing nor sound theology. *The Omega Code* was simultaneously a terribly-made film and proof positive, as a friend put it, that "Hollywood knows the Bible better than Christians do."

Artistic lodestones like *The Chronicles of Narnia*, *The Lord of the Rings* or *The Passion of the Christ* are rare gems precisely because their creators take a very high view of both faith and art. Lewis and Tolkien, in particular, were both members of "The Inklings," a group of artistic Oxford intellectuals who were devoted to the revitalization of faith-inspired literature. Both Lewis and Tolkien formulated and published detailed theories about the spiritual function of great literature. Both Lewis and Tolkien also took their faith most seriously.

And their work achieved greatness because they aimed high, both theologically and artistically.

Other stories of lesser ambition are not unspiritual; not at all. Russell Stover peanut butter cups—or those cheap knock-offs we tend to give our kids on Easter, thinking they don't know the difference—are a fine substitute when you just need a quick snack. And quick snacks are sometimes just what we need. Lewis and Tolkien, in fact, both argued that any story, well-told, is by nature spiritually satisfying, even if it's long on literature but short on spirituality or vice versa.

But *The Chronicles of Narnia* isn't spiritually satisfying simply because it's a collection of run-of-the-mill well-told stories. Neither is it satisfying simply because its spirituality—"gold," in the parlance of G. K. Chesterton—is so easy to find. The gold in some books, Chesterton would say, requires so much work to find that it ends up ignored; humanity "is not incidentally engaged, but eternally and systematically engaged," he observed, "in throwing gold into the gutter and diamonds into the sea."[†] And so, unthinkingly, we often miss the Christian theology inherent in the vast majority of Western art; further, we too easily dismiss the best of it as "pagan" or "occultic." Harry Potter and Middle-earth come easily to mind.

Narnia, though, is more like a jewelry shop dressed up like a candy store—so much so that it's often mistaken for nothing more than a candy store. But to do Narnia justice, we must approach it respectfully both as art and as spirituality.

But even if we accept the premise that *The Chronicles of Narnia* succeeds both as literature and as elucidation of Christian thought, we would be mistaken in presuming, then, that Lewis wrote with two aims. He only had one.

[†] G. K. Chesterton, *The Defendant*, p. 16.

A Unified Approach

Robert Frost wrote of "two roads" that "diverged in a yellow wood."[†] His metaphor, while potent, has led many to accept the notion that there are always only two roads from which to choose; and further, possibly mistaking Frost's intent, that the "road less traveled" is always the right choice. If we are Christians, this is only natural. Christ, after all, elaborated on the two roads of Hebrew Scripture: the wide way that leads to destruction and the narrow, winding, difficult path of salvation. So if we compare Christ's words to Frost's, they appear to be talking about the same things.

I don't believe they are.

Tolkien, in his essay "On Fairy Stories," also referenced Christ's words—but declared that fantasy, the "road to fairyland," is "not the road to Heaven; nor even to Hell."[‡] I have long found Tolkien's assertion troubling. What road is there in the middle, and where does it lead? Is Tolkien suggesting that fantasy, or art, is morally neutral? Further, is he suggesting that such moral neutrality is desirable?

On the contrary, I believe that Tolkien was subtly suggesting that effective fantasy—in fact, all great art—is a sublime meeting of the human and the divine. It is the magical place where men may encounter Faerie.

But salvation is still salvation; we are either on an ever-narrowing path toward God or on an ever-widening path away from Him. Yet art is not salvation.

There is, in fact, a fourth way with art, one that demands that we walk two roads at once: precisely what Frost's narrator wished to do. We cannot assume that one road is preferable to the other—that we must on the one hand emphasize spirituality at the cost of literary analysis, or on the other hand slavishly explicate art while ignoring its spiritual significance. And we also dare not assume, as Christians, that art is best appreciated by ignoring

---

[†] Robert Frost, "The Road Not Taken."

[‡] J. R. R. Tolkien, "On Fairy Stories," *The Tolkien Reader*, p. 34.

both of these aspects equally. There is no middle road. The third path is an illusion.

The Task of Walking Both Roads

What we must attempt is the appreciation of art both at the level of secular, human (if divinely-inspired) achievement and at the level of spiritual truth. And this is a dual appreciation, not a simultaneous one.

For Lewis and Narnia, then, we must realize that the author's object was faith, and his instrument was literature. He played a beautiful spiritual tune, if you will, with words. Walking both roads together means paying proper attention both to issues of faith, as expressed in the *Chronicles*, and to the literary means used to tell to tell the stories.

To clarify: if we mistakenly presume that *The Chronicles of Narnia* was conceived, or is best apprehended, through a simplistic, single-minded goal, we might equally well presume that Dvorak's *New World Symphony* is best appreciated through a spiritual analysis—or that the spirit of Scripture may be best derived through the intellectual rigor of our hermeneutics. But the musicality of a symphony may be dissected without doing violence to, and while still granting audience to, its deeper artistic meaning; likewise, the spiritual mystery of Scripture does not preclude, nor exist wholly independently of, exhaustive attention to the vagaries of Hebrew and Greek grammar.

I must further clarify here that I am not attempting to drag Scripture down to the level of mere human art. Not at all. Rather, I am attempting to raise our expectations of art nearer the level of the divine, as did Tolkien and Lewis.

By way of analogy, let us compare *The Chronicles of Narnia* and the Bible. I have already remarked that the object of Lewis' *Chronicles* was faith, and that his instrument was literature. The object of the Bible, on the other hand, is the Word—that is, the Christ—and its instrument is words. Scripture is divine Truth expressed in human language.

If we think that we can divine God's meaning without understanding the words in which it is presented, we are fooling ourselves. Conversely, if we think that the very Body and Blood of Christ can be tamed or fully contained by human words, we do not understand what we have come to. We have "not come to a mountain that can be touched and that is burning with fire; to darkness, gloom and storm," as the writer of Hebrews says. No. Instead, we "have come to Mount Zion, to the heavenly Jerusalem, the city of the living God." We have "come to thousands upon thousands of angels in joyful assembly, to the church of the firstborn, whose names are written in heaven... to God, the judge of all men, to the spirits of righteous men made perfect, to Jesus the mediator of a new covenant."[†] No small thing, indeed.

The Bible would fail if there were no real meaning behind it; and whatever meaning it might have would be lost if it were, to be candid, boring. But the fact is that The Good Book happens to be a good book. Strike that—it's a great book.

And now the analogy comes full circle. If we also think that we can divine Lewis' thoughts on faith without understanding the literary form in which those thoughts are presented, we are fooling ourselves. And if we think that Aslan and all that he represents can be tamed by our petty criticisms of Lewis' literary gaffes, we also do not understand what we have come to. We might as well join Shift, the Ape of *The Last Battle*, in rather smugly thinking that the stable is empty—when both Tash and Aslan may be found within.

So while we grant that Lewis had only one aim, just as God only had one aim with Scripture, why would we prefer to simple-mindedly analyze *The Chronicles of Narnia* only as literature? Or why would we equally simple-mindedly think that Narnia is best served by glibly summarizing the spiritual values to be found within its borders? Or worse—why would we think that it's possible to do justice to both aspects simultaneously?

[†] Hebrews 12:18-24.

Introduction

Maximizing Enjoyment of the Journey

In this volume, our introduction to the seven episodes in the *Chronicles* offers an example of how we may discard the smug assumption that we have chosen the road less traveled—an example of how we may take the difficult middle path which treats each work of art first as literature, and also as Christian enlightenment.

But we won't mix the two. You will see the difference between the two approaches side by side. The result, we think you will find, will be an increased appreciation of how each approach complements the other.

Oh—and we also expect that, as with a Reese's Peanut Butter Cup, you'll find that the flavor of the whole is enhanced by being able to distinguish the taste of each.

But if you find that you like the flavor of what we've done, you'll most likely enjoy reading—or rereading—*The Chronicles of Narnia* even more. There's no substitute for the Real Thing.

❧ In the Beginning... ❧

Synopsis by Jenn Wright

Digory Kirke has had to move with his terminally ill mother from a beautiful country home to his aunt and uncle's house in London. His father is away and his bed-ridden mother is gravely ill, so he is delighted to have found a friend when Polly Plummer, a next door neighbor, pops up.

One rainy day, Digory and Polly follow a tunnel-like passageway between the houses in their row. A miscalculation causes them to enter the attic room of Digory's Uncle Andrew. Andrew cons Polly into reaching for a brightly colored ring—and she disappears. He then cunningly plays on Digory's honor, pointing out that unless Digory goes after her (with two "return trip" rings), Polly is doomed. Digory angrily complies.

After putting on another ring, he emerges from a shallow pool into a peaceful, sleepy, wooded place, where Polly is resting languidly by a tree. After a few moments of "remembering" each other and how they got there, they don their rings and jump into a different pool—one that transports them to another world: Charn. The sun is old and tired-looking; everything is cold, dry, dusty. Polly and Digory enter a building filled with fine statues. On a pedestal sits a small bell, with a similarly small hammer next to it. An inscription warns that both ringing and not ringing the bell carry dire consequences; so Digory rings the bell.

Suddenly a tall, wickedly beautiful woman addresses them. She is Jadis, the queen of Charn, and the spell cast upon her world has been broken at the ringing of the bell. Believing the children to be spectacular magicians, she demands that they take her to their world so she can conquer it, too. Digory and Polly don their magic rings to flee the witch-queen; but she tags along, joining them in the Wood Between the Worlds.

Here, Jadis becomes weak, and the children are less intimidated by her. As they are about to don the "London" rings,

Two Roads through Narnia

Digory hesitates while abandoning Jadis to her death—once again allowing the witch to piggy-back passage with them.

When they emerge once again into Uncle Andrew's attic laboratory, chaos breaks loose. Believing Andrew to be a Great Magician, Jadis issues demands that Andrew is slobberingly happy to try to satisfy. But Jadis is impatient, and she hijacks the horse-drawn cab Uncle Andrew has procured and sets out on her conquest. Meanwhile, Digory frantically formulates plans to return the witch to her own world before she does more damage.

When the cab returns, a crowd follows. Jadis wrecks the cab, rips off the iron arm of a lamppost, and bashes a police officer on the head with it. Digory grabs the witch while Polly is touching both him and her ring, and together they snatch Jadis back into the Wood Between the Worlds—along with Frank, the cabby; his horse, Strawberry; and a simpering Uncle Andrew. Strawberry unknowingly steps into one the of the pools for a drink, and when Digory and Polly grab their green rings, the whole group is then transported through the pool to a dark world—a world at the moment of its creation.

We are now privy to the very creation of Narnia—a world sung into being by Aslan, a great Lion. Most in the group hearLthe lion singing the most beautiful song, as plants and creatures spring into being. But Jadis, in fear and anger, attempts to destroy Aslan by braining him with the broken-off arm of the lamppost; though she makes solid contact, the chunk of iron falls harmlessly to the ground. Jadis flees (but the lamppost arm grows into the famous beacon of Narnia's Lantern Waste).

Meanwhile, Aslan chooses a council of speaking animals, explaining to them that the humans present have brought evil into their brand new world. Digory, feeling terrifically ashamed, is yet hopeful that the great Lion might hold the cure for his mother. He approaches Aslan, and Aslan's eyes fill with anguished tears over Digory's pain and his mother's condition.

But Aslan doesn't grant Digory a miracle. Instead, he asks if the boy is prepared to undo the evil he brought into Narnia. At Digory's affirmative reply, Aslan tasks him with retrieving the

The Magician's Nephew

seed for a tree that will protect Narnia from the evil queen. Digory and Polly mount the newly-winged Fledge (a.k.a. Strawberry) to find—you guessed it—the apple from which the seed will be taken. Two days' flight later, they arrive at a gated courtyard on a hill, where a tree bearing large silver apples awaits Digory. Entering the courtyard, he finds a second written warning—that he should take of the fruit only for others, not for himself, lest he find his "heart's desire and find despair."[†] After plucking a single apple from the tree, he looks up to find Jadis, who has already consumed many apples. She tempts Digory to take the apple straight to his mother rather than back to Aslan. And Digory *is* tempted; but the witch tries to convince him to leave Polly behind as well. Digory comes to his little-boy senses and rides with Polly back to Aslan in determined obedience.

Still, Aslan doesn't allow him to take the apple back to his mother. Instead, the Lion asks him to throw the life-giving apple as far as he can. And he does, as Aslan's talking animals celebrate the coronation of King Frank the cabby and Queen Helen his wife (whom Aslan has miraculously brought to Narnia).

Meanwhile, the discarded apple has become an enormous tree. Aslan explains that its fruit will keep Jadis away, for the apples that she greedily ate have become simultaneously the thing she most loves and most despises. "All get what they want," Aslan counsels; "they do not always like it."[‡]

At this point, Digory understands that eating an apple from that tree for the wrong reasons at the wrong time will produce untold anguish and misery—and his hopes for his mother's health are dashed. However, Aslan is the creator of the apples, and an apple given by its creator is not the same as one purloined by a created being. Thus the story of *The Lion, the Witch and the Wardrobe* is germinated: with a solitary silver apple mercifully granted to a willful boy to take back to London for his ailing mother.

[†] C. S. Lewis, *The Magician's Nephew*, p. 157.
[‡] Ibid., p. 174.

15

∾ Magic: Characters and Lands ∾

Literary Analysis by George Rosok

Perhaps it's best, when reading *The Magician's Nephew*, to come at C. S. Lewis' Narnia series as a novice. The only other volume of the series that I had previously read was *The Lion, the Witch and the Wardrobe*, and that was many years ago. Given that I remembered little of it, and that I had read none of the other stories, I had the relative luxury of approaching *The Magician's Nephew* without bias.

That's a luxury, you ask? Not a handicap? Yes—without prior knowledge or understanding of the series as a whole, analysis of this book is less likely to be colored by what takes place in the other stories. And I'm sure there will be other newcomers like me whose interest has been piqued by the release of the Disney-produced film adaptation of *The Lion, the Witch and the Wardrobe*. Like me, they may be exploring opportunities to learn more about the Narnia series and to share their observations.

This essay specifically discusses how *The Magician's Nephew* comes across as a piece of children's literature in a time when the genre is dominated by the likes of Harry Potter and Lemony Snicket. To frame this discussion I'll focus on what I see as the common denominator in the story—magic. We will look at the role magic plays for each of the main characters, how it affects each of them, and, finally, what it offers us, today's readers.

Does this portrayal of magic have a chance of interesting us as much as the image of Harry Potter zooming around the sky on a magic broom during a rousing match of Quidditch? Perhaps not. I have to admit that, while I enjoyed *The Magician's Nephew*, it was often because it felt peacefully nostalgic—not because I was anxiously turning the page to see what happened next. But then, I'm not a kid anymore, either.

But I do think it's hard for *The Magician's Nephew* to compete against *Harry Potter*. The magic used in this story is not as fantastic as that which children today are used to. A ring used to pop from one world to another is a bit of a yawn compared to what kids see every day in movies and TV programs now. In fact, the pace of the entire story is slow and rather quaint, with the narrator occasionally inserting himself like a friendly old uncle. The point here, though, isn't the magic itself—and certainly not that friendly uncle. The point is that through the magic—perhaps in spite of it—the characters display their qualities, both good and bad.

So who has magic in *The Magician's Nephew*? How is it used and who benefits from the use of it? In the story most of the characters are touched by magic. Many wield it to some degree or another.

Andrew is the titular magician, but isn't much of one. Only by means of inheritance has he come to possess the substance from which the magic rings are made. Intrigued by the potential benefits and profits of magic, Andrew is too much of a coward to experiment on himself with the rings and instead uses helpless animals and children. When faced with those who really do possess magic, however, *he* is helpless. He views Jadis with fear, although he is attracted by her beauty and power. He sees Aslan only as Aslan physically appears, a wild beast, and Andrew has no conception of the power that Aslan wields.

The children, Polly and Digory—portrayed at first as naïve and mischievous—grow during the story to become brave, noble, patient and loving. They start out seeking adventure by attempting to explore an empty dwelling in their row of houses and wind up being forced to either mature or be overcome by the events that take place. The children also come to use the magic and are changed by it—not by the magic directly, as through some spell, but by the use and misuse of it by others in the story. Lewis portrays Digory as ultimately noble and courageous, although a bit impulsive. Polly is thoughtful and also brave. We quickly see that the two possess greater virtue in their innocence than does

Uncle Andrew in his "maturity."

When the children mistakenly enter Andrew's attic room and he discovers them, Lewis plainly displays Andrew's greed, cruelty, cowardice, manipulation and vanity. Sure, he is a magician of sorts, who must be fascinating to the children, but his use of magic is cruel and greedy—as he demonstrates when he tricks Polly into putting on the ring, forcing Digory to logically recognize that he must follow after her. This is precisely when Digory starts to show his mettle, and his behavior starts becoming an example for the reader.

The evil queen Jadis, whom Digory unwittingly brings back to life in the dying world of Charn, also uses magic as the source of her power, and through the use of it has destroyed her world. She is hungry to rule again. She is experienced in wielding magic and is overcome by the power of it. She does not have the strength of character to use it fairly for the greater good of all, but rather is only interested in using it to increase her domination and rule over as much and as many as possible.

Aslan wields the greatest magic in this story and possesses the greatest power. Aslan, alone, truly understands the power of the magic he wields. Although he does not appear to be the creator of the magic itself, he is very close to it. He has been given the magic to create Narnia, though, and through his wise use of such magic, it will be a wonderful, peaceful world for hundreds of years. But he also possesses a magical foresight, knowing that Narnia will not be able to withstand the evil of Jadis forever. Eventually he will be forced to deal with her. His strength and fairness are always evident, but so is the weight of this burden upon him.

In addition to the characters, the worlds they inhabit affect and are affected by the magic in this story. Until their disappearance from Andrew's attic, the children have been in London and, although it is a different era from our own, it is still familiar to the reader. The rings, by contrast, transport the children to a place that is unfamiliar to them *and* the reader—the Wood Between the Worlds. It is quiet and warm and full of life, and they are very comfortable there but oddly unaware of themselves, at first, or where they have come from. They are overcome by the bliss of the place, and indeed it might be viewed as heaven—a blissful place where specific forms may be just a way to give an earthly reference to the minds of Polly and Digory (and to us).

The Wood is beyond earthly conceptions of good. It is a place where evil does not exist and cannot survive. When Jadis is taken from her own world and brought there accidentally by the children, she simply withers. She loses all strength and seems to have no knowledge of herself or what she was before she came there. The appearance of Jadis in our own world is an indictment of sorts, in that she finds her strength, if not her magic, once again when she is taken to Earth. She sees Earth as a place of opportunity and is eager to rule it.

But Lewis serves up an indictment of other worlds, too. The children discover Charn when they (or Digory, at least) decide to do some grander exploring than what they had in mind when they set out to investigate the empty house in their row back in London. They determine the proper use of the rings and jump into one of the ponds in the Wood, then find themselves in a ruined and apparently uninhabited city. The sun is a dim red. The buildings are old and crumbling. Lewis describes it as deathly silent, not the warm, rich silence of the Wood Between the Worlds. After some exploring, they enter a great hall, where Digory is overcome by his curiosity and rings the bell that awakens Jadis. If Charn had ever been a fair and decent place, she and the people of Charn changed it into a place of power for power's sake, and she destroyed it when threatened with the possibility of losing that power to her sister. Later in the story, when they see that the pond that led to Charn is dried up, Aslan says that that world is ended as if it had never been. He warns that if the leaders of Earth do not change their path, Earth may have a similar fate.

Narnia fares somewhat better than Earth or Charn. We witness Narnia being created by the magic wielded by Aslan.

When the entire group is transported to this world, all is darkness. Aslan sings Narnia into existence. As they watch, light, mountains, rivers, trees, grass and animals all appear. Through this we begin to understand the true power of the magic and what Lewis is pointing to as the real source and meaning of it, both in the context of the story and metaphorically.

Of the characters, who understands the magic? Andrew is vain enough on Earth to suppose he is a great magician, but he understands it least of all. He wishes to use it for his own gain and is only a pretender. Jadis quickly sees this when she comes to Earth and drafts him to help her explore the virgin world she wishes to dominate. Andrew gains nothing from the magic and, if not for the strength of character of Polly and Digory and the beneficence of Aslan, he could easily have been destroyed by it.

Jadis understands the magic or, at least, that using it according to her will can make her very powerful, as she was on Charn. But through her misuse of it, she destroyed Charn and everyone living there. At the end of this story she remains in Narnia, but in a position that, for now, exerts no influence; she is in exile.

Aslan understands the magic and uses it toward the good for which it was intended. He also understands its power and danger and that using it, while granting great power, also places great responsibility on its user. Jadis and Andrew did not know this or did not care; destruction (in the case of Jadis) and mishap (in the case of Andrew) ensued.

Digory and Polly perhaps don't understand magic, but they are at least open-minded enough to see the dangers inherent in it. Digory craves it to save his dying mother, but is afraid to take it for his own use by stealing an apple. He doesn't know exactly what would happen, but he believes it would displease Aslan and fears the consequences. Because of his bravery and obedience, Digory is nonetheless awarded an apple by Aslan, which he is able to take it back to earth to miraculously cure his mother. Polly perhaps does not receive anything directly and serves mostly as a companion, but she grows much during the course of the story. In the end, even Uncle Andrew is restored to Earth and over time becomes redeemed. He does not become heroic, but after returning to Earth he at least becomes benign and attempts no more magic.

The peril of this story may be much more nuanced (read: *dull*) than what children today may be accustomed to, but the moral of the story and the virtues demonstrated within it are much more evident than in today's literature. Through the course of the story, the children grow, particularly Digory, and this prepares him for his greatest challenge. This challenge is not Jadis; she is merely one of the vehicles for it. The peril Digory faces is whether he can overcome the temptation to take one of the magic apples. This is made even more difficult because if it were only for himself he might easily overcome the temptation—but it is for his mother who is bed-ridden and dying back at their home in London.

Because he is able to overcome and win this battle with himself, we are presented with the lesson that selfless acts of strength and bravery can produce great outcomes. In this case, Digory is given one of the magical apples and is able to save his mother. Through this trial and all that has happened before, he has become a better human being. But in a world where we are accustomed to the sensory overload of physical peril that we see in movies, television programs, and even television news, we may have difficulty identifying emotionally with Digory's peril, even though the consequences of failure will result in his mother's premature death.

That is the problem for today's reader. Will Digory's triumph be appreciated or even understood in a world where the message of a story is easily overcome by the technology used to present it? I'm betting not.

❧ A Journey Toward the Creator ❧

Spiritual Commentary by Kathy Bledsoe

Five characters—standing in darkness on something cold, firm and seemingly barren and void—bear witness to the creation of the magical land of Narnia. Drawn into the experience by the sound of an exquisite and almost eerie singing that defies recognizable definitions of music, Digory, Polly, Frank the cabby, Uncle Andrew, Jadis the Witch Queen and Strawberry the horse are about to encounter the Creator. Each of them will take a different spiritual journey based on an individual response to both the music and the physical presence of the great Lion Aslan. What is the principal significance of this scene? And how does it help us interpret the spiritual signposts that author C. S. Lewis provides for his readers as the journey progresses?

Although this episode does not occur until the mid-point of *The Magician's Nephew*, it is truly where the journey begins. Through what they have experienced prior to this point, the characters have been given knowledge (or have recognized knowledge around them) that will determine their responses to Aslan, the story's personification of Jesus Christ. Some of them will embrace Aslan whole-heartedly, while others will avoid him completely. Some will joyfully become devoted disciples who will freely follow and do his will even in the face of suffering and death, while others will make their own rules, carve their own paths, pursue their own aggrandizement and continually instigate conflict by fighting against Aslan and all he represents. This tension between obedience and rebellion becomes a metaphor for the desire to know from whence we came—and the choice of what to do about what we discover.

The Bible tells us that planted deep within every person is the desire to know God. Though we—like the characters in this book—may choose to believe or reject what has been revealed to us, we would find it difficult to refute the seemingly universal and deep yearning to know why we exist and what our purpose is in life. How did we get here? Why were we put in this place and time? What are we supposed to do with this life? These are the questions that constantly beset and drive us.

Digory, for example, in early conversations with the amoral and self-serving Uncle Andrew, shows himself to be a young moral and ethical apologist, who quite reveals Uncle Andrew to be the villain that he is. How did Digory get this way? Was his conscience developed over time by equally moral and ethical parents? If so, where did they learn or from whom? One may argue nature and nurture or trial and error, but both intuition and science tell us that there is a beginning to all things—a point of creation. Thus, the search for the creator or "prime mover" begins.

As Digory and the others listen to the music and watch the creation of light in Narnia, they are stricken with an inexplicable recognition to which they just can't quite give a name. This is the call of that inner yearning to know... the response to the creator's voice planted deep within the soul.

For Digory, Polly, Frank and Strawberry, this call is welcomed and brings great joy and a desire to know more, and more fully. Jadis and Uncle Andrew, on the other hand, are horrified. Uncle Andrew wants to find a hole to crawl into and hide. Jadis is so angered by a power that exceeds hers that she would rather destroy everything than endure existence in such a wretched place.

Each of these responses is typical of the God-given right each of us has been granted to choose what our relationship with the Creator will be. C. S. Lewis knew this journey intimately, having struggled well into adulthood before completing his discovery of that needed relationship on a dark and solitary walk one evening after years of debate with such devout men as J. R. R. Tolkien. Lewis recognized that this encounter with the Creator, shared by himself and his characters, launches the real journey.

Once this foundational journey is understood, we can pay

true attention to other spiritual themes that Lewis weaves into the pages of *The Magician's Nephew*. The most distinct is Narnia's metaphorical creation itself. Beginning with a dark void, Lewis faithfully follows the Genesis story as Aslan calls forth vegetation and animals. The story is a story, of course, and not meant to be a rote reiteration of the Biblical myth. Aslan dubs the Cabby and his wife (who is pulled out of her own world into Narnia) King Frank and Queen Helen, not Adam and Eve, and they are given dominion over Narnia and its inhabitants—and responsibility for naming the animals and plants, just as God instructed Adam and Eve to do in Genesis. Aslan also commands King Frank to make his living from the earth; blesses Frank and Helen and their children and grandchildren; and promises that their offspring will be kings of Narnia and of neighboring Archenland. The promises of Aslan echo the promises God makes to Abraham in Genesis— that he will be the father of offspring more numerous than the stars.

As a sidebar to the creation of Narnia, Lewis also notes mankind's destructive tendency to misuse creation. Uncle Andrew looks at Narnia and sees the burgeoning life and beauty in terms of pounds and shillings. First on his agenda is Aslan's death, so that he can develop Narnia and possibly live forever.

Lewis now has Aslan expand on another theme that has run through the book since the first pages—the existence of good and evil in the world and the resultant and inevitable conflict this creates. Just as God confronted Adam and Eve after they ate the forbidden fruit, Aslan turns to confront Digory, who is responsible for bringing the evil and powerful Queen Jadis from Charn—a dead world that she has misruled into destruction—into the beautiful, new, vibrant and perfect Narnia. At first, Digory attempts to refocus Aslan's attention on Jadis, but Aslan quickly redirects Digory, reminding him that he is responsible for his actions and must now requite the wrong that he has committed. While God certainly never expects us to be responsible for another person's wrongdoing, the sad thing we come to realize (as does Digory) is that our wrongdoings and poor choices may have far-reaching consequences for those around us and the world in which we live—just as the choices of others also affect us. None of us live in a vacuum. Despite the best of intentions, Digory's own agenda—his own will and desire—has caused him to act impulsively, without considering how this might affect others. He just had to ring that bell, just as Eve had to try that fruit!

But how can we point a finger at Digory, or even Adam and Eve? We know, deep in our own hearts, that our desires and perceived needs—or just downright wants—drive us to make choices that we later recognize as ill-advised. How often have we heard out of our own mouths, "so-and-so or such-and-such made me do it?" And we also see that this is a typically human pattern. Digory's choice in ringing the bell out of self-gratification and curiosity echoes Polly's choice early in the book when she impulsively accepts the yellow ring from Uncle Andrew because the rings are the most beautiful and desirable objects that she has ever seen, and she covets them. Likewise, Uncle Andrew and Jadis are driven by their desire to possess and use power to their own ends. Their decisions are based solely on what's in it for them, and the rest of the universe be damned! In addition, when Jadis is not present, Uncle Andrew forgets his fear of her and reverts to his own plans of treachery. He is proof of our own inclination to dismiss the cost of wrong choices when any consequence seems far away or nonexistent. Lewis helps us realize that conflict comes from many quarters, even—or, perhaps, especially—from within. How might the choices we make today affect our world and those around us tomorrow—for good as well as for evil?

But wait, you say. Digory's motives are driven by his deep love for his mother and his desire to save her. Isn't this noble and right and selfless? Yes, and Aslan recognizes this in Digory, but even Digory sees that this part of himself also houses a dark side—a side that desires to take control and go its own way without regard for consequences. Aslan reminds Digory that he must count the cost before acting, no matter how noble the deed may seem on he surface.

Aslan assures Digory that good will eventually triumph,

but that Narnia will have to struggle through the battle between good and evil. The reality is that evil is present in the world, not as God ordained or desired, but as mankind invited by our own free choices. Digory mourns even as we say, "if only…" But God is not a puppeteer. He wants us to seek Him and meet Him without strings attached. No one is forced to know God.

What of this god, Aslan? What do we see in his character that draws Digory, Polly, Frank and Strawberry? The answer is found in Aslan's first command to the newly created world. As Aslan awakens Narnia, the first directive he gives them is to love. Those drawn to Aslan recognize that this command grows out of a foundational attribute deeply ingrained in the Creator. Primarily through Digory's interaction with Aslan, we witness the love that he has for all that he has made and knows. When Digory courageously looks into Aslan's eyes after asking that his mother be cured, he sees that Aslan's anguish over his pain (and hers) is even deeper than his own.

But those repelled by Aslan—namely Jadis and Andrew—have no love save that of self-preservation. Their hearts are so hard that they find his song discordant and grating, and only seek to run away. Again, none is forced to respond; Jadis and Andrew are allowed to make their own choices.

Justice is also an attribute of this Narnian god. Though he has the power to destroy evil with a single breath, he allows Jadis to remain. There will be an ultimate confrontation between this all-powerful good and her venomous evil, but it will come in Aslan's time, according to his plan, and dependent upon his will. He will allow circumstances to develop in Narnia until the time is ripe to bring a new reality. He alone will choose the time and place to redeem Narnia. And he has determined that Adam's race (mankind)—having brought the evil in through personal choice—must help to correct this wrong.

God's right to decide and do as He pleases with His creation (referred to as His sovereignty, His kingly and royal prerogative) has always been a thorny issue with humans. As Lewis demonstrates with Uncle Andrew, we all have a strong desire to direct our own lives and have our own way and mete out our own justice. Thus the eternal conflict within us: Be our own god, or let God be God?

Lewis also does a thorough job of exploring temptation in *The Magician's Nephew*. Within the first few pages of the book, we are aware of a room in Digory's house that, according to Aunt Letty, must never be entered. Just as God forbade Adam and Eve to eat from the tree of the knowledge of good and evil, Uncle Andrew has forbidden anyone to enter the room where he works to perfect his magic. Of course, this is immediately intriguing to Digory and Polly: temptation number one. And even though they do not intentionally set out to seek this particular room, their errant arithmetic—used to determine the distance to the empty house through the connected attics—gains them access, by their own choice to open the door in the brick wall. Polly allows her curiosity to overcome her and chooses to be the first to enter the room even though she knows that this is not the abandoned dwelling they were seeking.

Temptation number two: stay and explore, or get out. Digory knows that it is wrong to remain, but Polly has spotted the gorgeous yellow and green rings, and her desire to know more about them moves her into the role of leader: temptation number three. She leads Digory far enough into the room that Uncle Andrew (who has been biding his time waiting for them) is able to lock both doors and entrap them.

Through flattery and deceptive logic, Uncle Andrew manipulates each child just as the serpent in the Garden of Eden manipulated Eve. He recognizes that the moral force in Digory may be hard to overcome, so he focuses on Polly and her natural attraction to the rings. Just as the snake encouraged Eve to pick the fruit, Uncle Andrew entices Polly to touch one of the rings and wham! she is spirited out of her world.

Following a many-paged discussion of morals and ethics (Digory has them, Uncle Andrew does not), Digory is led into his own personal temptation to rescue Polly because Uncle Andrew assaults his honor. Won't Digory rescue the lady, as is the manly thing to do? His choice to go after her (and who would not make that choice with him?) begins the story that Lewis ultimately took seven books to complete.

In the land of Charn, Digory is also tempted, out of defiance and competition, to strike the bell. And finally, in a certain garden at the top of a certain hill in Narnia, Digory faces the ultimate temptation.

Aslan has sent Digory to obtain the special apple which, when planted in Narnia, will produce a tree that protects the land with one hundred years of peace. Jadis, just as the serpent did with Eve, entices Digory to take the life-giving apple to his mother—to use the rings, forsaking all in Narnia to return to her and his world. And this time, Digory really understands that his choices have affected the course of events, and with the maturity of experience, he makes the choice for Aslan and not Jadis—the choice for good rather than evil—even though the path for good will be harder to tread than the path of evil.

From encounters with the Creator to temptation and the nature of good and evil in the world, *The Magician's Nephew* provides a great and entertaining foundation for the discussion of spiritual topics, with children as well as adults. Written in a vernacular that they can enjoy, and couched in the genre of fantasy that they love, the book brings forth profound and deep topics that should not be ignored in childhood yet are often shunted aside because an adult doesn't know where or how to begin the discussion. And though there is more than enough to talk about in this book, six more wait to entertain and enlighten.

Aslan closes the first story with a promise to Digory. Because he has made the correct choice, Digory will see his mother healed—not for eternity in their world, but for the length of her life. Aslan also promises redemption for Narnia—the price of which Aslan himself will pay. But that is were the journey continues...

The Lion, the Witch and the Wardrobe

This is what all the fuss is about.

Published as the first volume of *The Chronicles of Narnia*, this story introduces us to C. S. Lewis' wardrobe, a literary device perhaps as well known as Lewis Carroll's looking glass or Aladdin's lamp. Certainly the most famous of the Narnian children's stories, it is also perhaps the most controversial.

Why? Because it is the foundation upon which the success of the Chronicles rests—and this foundation explicitly retells the heart of the Christian story. In Narnia, as in the Bible, an omnipotent Maker offers His Son as a living sacrifice in payment for the sins of the Sons of Adam.

Many tales present a Christ figure. In *The Lord of the*

Rings, for instance, Gandalf gives his life to save the Fellowship on the Bridge of Khazad-dum. In this tale, however, Aslan's sacrifice is not just symbolically suggestive. As with Christ in the Bible, Aslan doesn't merely die to save lives; he dies as a substitutionary payment for sin. And Aslan is scourged and mocked in much the same manner as the biblical soldiers abuse Jesus.

So why is the book controversial? Atheists see this tale as a Christian sneak-attack, an attempt to poison the minds of young children with mystical mumbo-jumbo. Many Christians, meanwhile, are troubled because Lewis freely incorporates pagan imagery into his tale as well. And, of course, it's a tale about witches and magic. We are not here, of course, overly concerned about these controversies.

After George reviews the basic plot of *The Lion, the Witch and the Wardrobe*, our analysis and commentary will instead focus on aspects of the story less frequently examined. First, Kathy addresses some of the more curmudgeonly assessments of the book's literary merits; then Jenn offers insight into some of the spiritual issues that lay beneath the more obvious allegorical features of the text.

We apologize in advance to those desiring a fuller explication of the story's Christ allegory; but plenty has been written on that subject to date, and can be easily found elsewhere.

ഏ Into the Wardrobe ༀ

Synopsis by George Rosok

Peter, Susan, Edmund and Lucy Pevensie are sent from London to an old professor's country house because of dangerous German air raids during World War II. One rainy day they go exploring and find a room that is empty except for a large wardrobe. Lucy, the youngest, looks into the wardrobe and climbs in among several long fur coats. She walks until she feels trees and snowy ground instead of coats and a wooden floor.

Seeing a light ahead, she walks further and discovers that it is a lamppost in a forest. A faun by the name of Tumnus steps out from the trees, informing her that she is in the land of Narnia. Innocent and trusting, she accepts his invitation to tea. At his home, Tumnus tells Lucy many stories of the forest and plays a strange flute, the tune of which makes her want to both dance and sleep. She eventually rouses herself and prepares to leave, but Mr. Tumnus begins crying, confessing to Lucy his involvement with the White Witch, who has ordered him to kidnap any human he sees. He admits to luring her to his cave, intending to lull her to sleep with his music, then turn her over to the witch. His true good nature re-emerges, however, and instead he helps Lucy back through the forest to the lamppost, where she finds her way back through the wardrobe.

Upon returning, Lucy jumps out of the wardrobe. Though it seems to her that she was gone for hours, she finds out that she was only gone a moment. She has not been missed! She tells her older siblings about Narnia, but, naturally, they think she is making it up. Edmund, the next oldest, teases her mercilessly.

The next time the children play hide-and-seek inside, Lucy climbs into the wardrobe to avoid the seeking Edmund. He also climbs in, expecting to find Lucy. Instead, he finds the snowy wood in Narnia. A reindeer-drawn sled driven by a dwarf appears. On a seat behind the dwarf is a very tall, beautiful woman dressed

31

in white fur and holding a long, gold wand. Edmund is captivated.

The White Witch uses a smooth voice and magic candy to trick the boy into telling her all about Lucy, the faun, Peter and Susan. After the witch leaves, Lucy and Edmund find each other. Lucy is overjoyed now that Edmund can confirm her stories of Narnia to the others; but when they return Edmund lies and tells Peter and Susan that he and Lucy were pretending.

Peter and Susan go to the professor for help, and are more than surprised when he suggests that Lucy might be telling the truth. Later, on another rainy day, all four children climb into the wardrobe to avoid a sightseeing party touring the old house. They discover that Lucy's stories are true when they all find themselves in the snowy wood. Lucy leads them to Mr. Tumnus' cave, where they are distressed to find Mr. Tumnus gone and his tidy home wrecked. He has been arrested by the witch's chief of secret police.

The children wonder what to do—until they meet Mr. Beaver. He tells them that the Great Lion, Aslan, may be in Narnia. They don't know who Aslan is, but all of them, save Edmund, feel wonderful at the sound of his name. Mr. Beaver cautiously leads them back to his den where he and his wife explain a Narnian prophecy: When four human children sit upon the thrones in the castle at Cair Paravel, the witch's wintry reign will end and she will die. They must meet Aslan at the Stone Table as quickly as possible—the witch intends to kill the children, thus preventing the prophecy from coming true.

But Edmund has gone. Mr. Beaver suggests that Edmund has gone to the witch. They must leave immediately.

Edmund makes his way to the witch's castle, where he finds her courtyard full of stone creatures. The witch is angry to discover that he has not brought his siblings to her. She dispatches her secret police to the Beavers' den to kill anyone there.

Meanwhile, the Beavers and the children hide in a secret hollow. In the morning, they hear bells and worry it might be the witch's sled; instead, they find that it is Father Christmas. The witch's hold on Narnia is weakening. Father Christmas gives them each gifts including a sword and shield for Peter, a horn for Susan, and a small liquid-filled bottle for Lucy.

Meanwhile, Edmund has been forced to sit with the witch as her sled covers mile after mile through the forest. In the morning they come upon a party of forest creatures enjoying a feast that Father Christmas has given them. The enraged witch turns the whole party to stone. But Edmund notices it is getting warmer. The snow is melting. The sled can no longer move.

The other children and the Beavers enjoy the spring that is blossoming around them. As the sun goes down, they climb a hill; at the top they find the Stone Table, a gray slab supported by four stone posts. Aslan is there amongst a crowd of creatures, including two leopards who carry his crown and standard.

Eventually Peter moves forward and Aslan welcomes them. Aslan calmly asks where the fourth child is, and Mr. Beaver shares his speculation that Edmund has gone over to the White Witch. Aslan then takes Peter to the edge of the hilltop and shows him the castle where he will be king. Suddenly they hear Susan's horn. Peter rushes off and finds her being chased into a tree by Fenris Ulf. He slays the wolf with his sword, but another wolf escapes.

The escaped wolf reports back to the witch, who summons all her people to fight. As she is about to kill Edmund, Aslan's eagles and centaurs arrive and rescue the boy, but the witch escapes.

The next morning when Peter, Susan and Lucy wake, they find Edmund talking with Aslan; Edmund then sincerely apologizes to his family. But the witch arrives, reminding Aslan of the Deep Magic within Narnia: Every traitor belongs to her—so Edmund's life is forfeit by law.

After a private discussion with the witch, Aslan announces that she has given up her claim on Edmund. She is oddly joyful. Aslan, on the other hand, is quiet and stern. That night Susan and Lucy cannot sleep. They leave their tent and see Aslan walking into the woods. Following him, they see that he is taking the route back to the Stone Table. In a clearing he discovers them, but allows them to accompany him.

At the last tree before the hilltop, Aslan tells the girls to hide. From there they see the witch's people crowded around the Stone Table. Aslan walks proudly to the crowd, but the witch orders Aslan be tied. The crowd beats him, binds him, and drags him onto the table. The witch declares that the Deep Magic must be appeased, and that she will now rule Narnia forever. She raises her arm, and, as the girls cover their eyes, she slays Aslan with a stone knife.

Assured that Aslan is dead, the witch's horde rushes past the girls' hiding place. Susan and Lucy go to Aslan and stay with him until morning, when friendly mice gnaw away the ropes that bind him. The girls walk to the edge of the hilltop, and as the sun rises they hear a deafening crack. The Stone Table has been broken in two and Aslan is gone. But the girls are overjoyed to hear Aslan's voice. Though they think he may be a ghost, Aslan explains that, although the witch knew the Deep Magic, there is Deeper Magic that is even more powerful.

Susan and Lucy climb on Aslan's back and he runs to the witch's castle, where he restores the stone creatures in her courtyard and halls to life, simultaneously calling on them to fight the witch. After leaving the castle, they find Peter, Edmund and Aslan's army in a battle with the witch and her minions. With a great roar, Aslan jumps onto the witch; she is killed and her army quickly defeated.

The battle over, Peter tells Aslan that Edmund heroically destroyed the witch's wand. He was badly wounded doing it, however. Using the liquid from the bottle Father Christmas gave her, Lucy heals Edmund as well as others who were wounded in the fight. The next day, the children, Aslan and his people march to Cair Paravel. The children are crowned; Aslan quietly leaves. The children grow into Kings and Queens who govern Narnia well.

Many years later, Mr. Tumnus comes to tell them that the White Stag has been spotted—the White Stag who grants wishes if you catch him. The Kings and Queens hunt the stag, following it into a thicket, which the royal siblings find oddly familiar. They find the lamppost; as they continue walking, they discover they are no longer among trees but among long fur coats. Suddenly they tumble out of the wardrobe. They are mere children once more, and scarcely a moment has passed since they climbed in to hide from the sightseeing party.

Later they tell the professor the whole story and wonder if they might ever get back to Narnia. He tells them that they will not likely get back through the wardrobe. But they will return to Narnia someday—when they aren't looking for it, and when they least expect it.

❧ The Heart of a Child ❧

Literary Analysis by Kathy Bledsoe

The Lion, the Witch and the Wardrobe is pedantic, often trite and repetitive, allegorized *ad nauseum*, poorly edited, and shocking to find in the repertoire of an author of C. S. Lewis' caliber.

Now that I have your attention, allow me to explain why very little of the preceding statement is true.

Pedantry (here used as "unimaginative and pedestrian"—with apologies to Lemony Snicket!) is a term that might be applied to Lewis by the reader who has read *The Lion, the Witch and the Wardrobe* only once. But Lewis' juvenile writings are like the proverbial onion whose layers must be peeled away to reach the core. Just as the center of the onion often has the most concentrated flavor, the core of *The Lion, the Witch and the Wardrobe* yields fresh insights with each return to Narnia. Superficially read, the book might give the impression that it is just for children and thus be easily dismissed by adults as another piece of fantasy claptrap that only serves the purpose of getting the kiddies to drift off to sleep at night. We might even focus on the similarities we see with other works of children's fantasy and accuse Lewis of having no imagination of his own.

But what of the saying, "imitation is the highest form of praise"? Rather than calling Lewis unimaginative, we can praise the man for a mind that seems to have had the capacity to hold on to everything he had ever read. Lewis was naturally influenced by his experiences just as all of us are. It is not unimaginative plagiarism that causes Lewis to use a piece of furniture to invade the land of Narnia, but recognition that this device works. Why reinvent the wheel when a writing desk worked for George MacDonald, a looking glass sufficed for Lewis Carroll, and Barrie brought the delicious advent of pixie dust? And, as we are taught in college, the great author writes about what he knows.

The Lion, the Witch and the Wardrobe

Lewis and his brother Warnie spent hours as children "imagining" in a spare room containing a big old wardrobe.

If *The Lion, the Witch and the Wardrobe* is not pedantry, then, what is it? We will see below that, in writing about what he knew, Lewis managed to address the deep needs of humanity through a very personal expression of faith, using many literary devices—including allegory. In the process, Lewis provided a cathartic experience both for himself and for his readers.

The wardrobe itself, of course, is the key to how this all works. Upon repeat readings of the book, we begin to understand that the wardrobe is more than a piece of furniture and that its usage has rules. Yes, the wardrobe is a doorway into another world, but it cannot be used carelessly or at the whim of any individual. Lack of access to their own world (whether due to weather or the crowding of adults) makes Narnia available and accessible to the Pevensie children. Lewis, through the story, is decrying the necessity of a time that required the removal of children from their familiar surroundings because of the danger of falling bombs. The perils of war remained heavy upon Lewis' heart, as did the separation from his mother as a result of her untimely death when he was nine. The wardrobe becomes a way to escape and explore feelings too private to be shared otherwise.

For Lewis, there was good precedent for using fantasy to work out these ideas for both children and adults. In his essay, "On Three Ways of Writing for Children," Lewis says that "a children's story which is enjoyed only by children is a bad children's story."[†] He further offers that "there may be an author who at a particular moment finds not only fantasy but fantasy-for-children the exactly right form for what he wants to say."[‡] He was supported in these statements by his friend and fellow fantasy author, J. R. R. Tolkien, who felt that if fantasy "is worth reading

---

[†] C. S. Lewis, "On Three Ways of Writing for Children," *Of Other Worlds*, p. 24.
[‡] Ibid., p. 28.

at all it is worthy to be written for and read by adults."[†]

Fantasy satisfies something deep within the human being that wants to create worlds and desires to interact with those worlds in ways that have been denied in our real one. Narnia is Lewis' chance to participate in the creation of a land in which old tales can have different endings or may simply be explored to see why things have to happen the way they do. Animals talk, trees are alive, ideas are personified, time seems to stand still—all so that other things can be made sense of and explained. The great danger of fantasy, of course, is preferring the other worlds to our own; but Lewis brings his heroes and heroines back out of the wardrobe for reality checks. He does not allow his characters (or himself) the luxury of "hiding" forever in Narnia.

In really good literature, there comes a point where the reader recognizes that the soul of the author is being laid bare. One may not always understand what drove the writer to expose himself through his prose, but there is a delicious sense of being allowed into secret places where one is tantalized with suggestions of things too personal and perhaps painful to expose other than through the veil of literature. The heart of C. S. Lewis lies exposed in *The Chronicles of Narnia*, most especially in *The Lion, the Witch and the Wardrobe*, which becomes an outlet for the passion and the personal pain of a very private man.

Several of Lewis' biographers concede that he would have continued writing only theological books if it had not been for a fateful debate with Elizabeth Anscombe in 1948. Lewis had just finished his book *Miracles*, and Anscombe took him to task at a public meeting over his philosophical definition of naturalism in chapter three. Although she was not questioning his faith, Lewis' inability to answer her argument left him mortified and feeling like a failure. He resolved never to write another theological work so that he would never again be open to such humiliation. In addition, Lewis was in a constant search to understand the nature of God and the great gift he had been given because of Jesus

---

[†] J. R. R. Tolkien, "On Fairy Stories," *The Tolkien Reader*, p. 67.

Christ. So in many ways, the creation of Narnia can be understood as an outlet for a passionate, private man—one searching to find his Maker in a relationship that had relevance for both the Creator (God) and the creature (Lewis). Rereading *The Lion, the Witch and the Wardrobe* from this perspective brings the private man, Lewis, into sharper focus and presents good proof that there are indeed better ways of telling the truth than through mere argumentation.

Now we must turn to the issue of allegory. The following definition will suffice:

> Allegory is a form of extended metaphor in which objects, persons and actions in a narrative are equated with the meanings that lie outside the narrative itself. The underlying meaning has moral, social, religious or political significance, and characters are often personifications of abstract ideas as charity, greed or envy. Thus an allegory is a story with two meanings, a literal meaning and a symbolic meaning.[†]

Immediately upon reading the above definition, one might be led to say that Lewis does use the device too much. Lewis, in fact, embraced the use of allegory to such a degree that it disturbed his friend Tolkien, who abhorred the use of allegory and fought tooth and nail to keep people from finding it in any of his own "Fairy Stories." Nonetheless, as blatant as Lewis' use of allegory is, it works in this story for several reasons.

First, the use of allegory can enhance any story. How boring is it to read a story that only has one meaning? Multiple levels of meaning are what create a classic—a book to which we return over and over because there is always something new to find, or a new way to think about something because of ever-increasing progress in maturation. A twenty-something person doesn't view or think about the world the same way that a forty-

---

[†] Ted Nellen, www.tnellen.com/cybereng/lit_terms/allegory.html.

something person does—or as a child or teenager does.

Having read *The Lion, the Witch and the Wardrobe* in at least four different stages of life now, I can honestly admit that it has meant something different to me every time through it. Discussing the book with a ten-year-old is profoundly different from discussing it with a group of peers as a fifty-year-old. As Lewis himself said, "No book is really worth reading at the age of ten which is not equally (and often far more) worth reading at the age of fifty."[†]

Second, Lewis' use of allegory is completely blatant for good reason. There are no surprises and no guessing games as to what things could possibly mean. Lewis never stoops to the use of obscure references, theological language or confusing double entendre. (Okay, there is that one reference to Lilith; but was Lewis being snobbishly well-read, or just trying to throw in something for his more esoteric friends?) When the children are in Narnia, the entire story is a metaphorical children's Bible. Lewis capitalizes the nouns which refer to Aslan just as the pronouns for Jesus are capitalized in the Bible. Aslan is a Lion, a clear reference to one of Jesus' messianic titles—the Lion of Judah. The stone table is decorated with pagan etchings, a place of sacrifice as pagan as the cross used by the Romans to kill Jesus. Queen Jadis is the personification of evil and, although not an exact representation of Satan, close enough to elicit the comparison. Edmund on one level is just a bratty little kid, but on another embodies greed, self-serving behavior and disdain for the consequences of his actions for himself or others. Aslan willingly gives up his own life for Edmund, who is not worthy of the sacrifice. Mr. Tumnus, the faun, is the Judas who betrays the presence of the children to Queen Jadis, which ultimately leads to the capture of Aslan. Even Father Christmas is included. And what child doesn't recognize Father Christmas as the God-like giver of good gifts? Such examples are countless and provide the opportunity for discussion on almost any artistic and intellectual

---

[†] C. S. Lewis, "On Stories," *Of Other Worlds*, p. 15.

level imaginable.

Third, the use of allegory doesn't mean that the comparisons have to be exact. After all, we are talking fantasy fiction, and the author has the prerogative of creating and composing his own tale. For instance, Queen Jadis may display many of the character traits known of Satan, but Lewis leads us more toward a personified evil than an exact duplication of a stereotypical character. Similarly, Aslan doesn't die on a cross, yet his sacrifice is every bit as poignant and relevant within the context of this story as Jesus' is in His. This is what Tolkien called "a recognition of fact, but not a slavery to it."[†]

And this leads us to the cathartic nature of the story. If we are to find reading the tale worthy of our time and relevant to our lives, we must trust the author to use what works—such as allegory—and allow him that artistic license. After all, a great part of the satisfaction of writing is found in the purification or purging of the emotions; that is, catharsis. Lewis' use of allegory in his story allows for the release of his disillusionment, disappointment and personal grief. We must allow Lewis to be Lewis, forcing him to neither "laugh at" nor "explain away" the magic of the tale (to once again use Tolkien's words[‡]).

Ultimately, we recognize that *The Lion, the Witch and the Wardrobe* has accomplished well the four elements Tolkien considered essential for the fairy story: "Fantasy, Recovery, Escape, Consolation."[§] The book is good because we are free to become children without losing our identities as adults. Each of us is encouraged to have the open and accepting heart of a child—one easily lost as we become jaded by our world.

While both Tolkien and Lewis agreed that fantasy could be a realm left for children, they believed that older people were probably most desperately in need of recovery, escape and consolation. I would personally neither separate fantasy from

---

[†] J. R. R. Tolkien, "On Fairy Stories," *The Tolkien Reader*, p. 75.

[‡] Ibid., p. 39.

[§] Ibid., p. 67.

adults nor the other three from children.

In the exercise of our imaginations we can find relief from the constant pressures of our world. Reading fantasy is the purest use of imagination aside from writing and creating it ourselves. It does not matter that our individual mental pictures of Aslan aren't the exact mental picture that Lewis had of him. In sharing the fantasy, we become co-creators with Lewis and experience a partnership in a different world where problems may be confronted, worked on, and finally talked about and resolved for the benefit of the real world. The individual imaginations meet to compare, discuss and grow. Books are the best vehicles for this exercise because the reader is not at the mercy of anyone else's visualization of the story. How many of us, after all, have not been disappointed at some time in a screenwriter's or director's visual interpretation of a favorite story? Precious few.

Recovery—the need to take a step back to regain a fresh view and make a new start—is needed by all people, although it could be conceded that children do not have enough life experience to necessitate fresh starts. However, if as adults we don't take the time to stop and think about what we believe and why we believe it, we are in real danger of stagnation and decay. Lewis' use of allegory proves to be a very non-threatening way to explore some hard topics, such as fear, death, suffering, pain, love and commitment.

Only a very foolish or hypocritical person would deny the need for escape—which does not mean desertion, but rather a break to be able to assess where one is and appropriate the necessary means to recover the clear view. Remember that Lewis did not allow the four children to remain forever in Narnia, but took them back and forth through the wardrobe at different times and for different reasons.

Lastly, a good story provides consolation, i.e., the happy ending. This is what Tolkien coined "the Eucatastrophe"—the good catastrophe—that "denies ... universal defeat" and brings

"Joy beyond the walls of the world."[†] We don't always get to have happy endings in our lives, but if we lose the hope of an ultimately happy ending we can easily give up the need for imagining, recovery and escape, making life meaningless and empty. Lewis regained his own child-like heart by opening a wardrobe door to another world, and he generously invites those who would read to come along.

Before concluding, I must briefly address two more parts of my opening salvo.

First, poor editing is just a fact we have to accept about Lewis, and is the only criticism that cannot be argued against in *The Lion, the Witch and the Wardrobe*. C. S. Lewis rapped out the seven books in this series between 1950 and 1957. He obviously was not the slave to detail that Tolkien was and showed more interest in getting the story out there than in noticing whether the pronouns for Mr. Tumnus in one chapter match the pronouns for Mr. Tumnus in the next. Only the literature majors really pick up on such things (anyone else needing their perceptions validated?).

And finally, many critics of Lewis' juvenile fiction have accused him of the repetition of phrases and the overuse of some words and ideas, citing these "failures" as proof of poor writing. (As discussed above, the use of allegory falls into the supposedly-trite category.) But obviously, the man who was capable of writing books such as *Mere Christianity*, *The Screwtape Letters,* and *Surprised by Joy* was not at a loss for words. In fact, Tolkien actually became miffed at Lewis' productivity and accused him of being too prolific a writer.

But the continued popularity of both Lewis' nonfiction and his fiction, long after his death, proves that people find what Lewis has to say relevant. It would be wise to remember that even though these Narnian tales were written for all ages to enjoy, the primary target reader was a child, or at least a reader who could

---

[†] J. R. R. Tolkien, "On Fairy Stories," *The Tolkien Reader*, p. 85f.

enter into the story with the heart of a child. The repetition of a phrase like "It is very silly to shut oneself into a wardrobe" actually makes sense when we think about human nature. All but the most profoundly exceptional children have to hear the same admonitions and instructions over and over again before they finally learn. Those who have raised children have heard themselves say, "How often do I have to repeat myself?" more times than they care to count.

And this tendency toward "deafness" is not limited to children. As adults, we find constant repetition in our workplaces, homes, churches—anywhere something significant has to be accomplished. Repetition may be annoying, but that is how a human being learns.

❧ The Heart of an Adult ❧

Spiritual Commentary by Jenn Wright

It would be far too easy (pedantic, really) to re-illuminate the basic spiritual allegory of this first-born of the Narnia Chronicles, in which Aslan is Jesus and Jadis is Satan and the parallel salvation story is wrapped up neatly with a silver string.

But this is Lewis—a phenomenal Christian mind, an outstanding philosopher, a prolific, renowned author of works ranging from children's books to science fiction to treatises on grief to thorough apologetics of the Christian faith. Given all of that, we can safely assume that there is more to *The Lion, the Witch and the Wardrobe* than just the "basic" allegory. After all, if that were really all there were to it, why would six other books be necessary to complete the story?

First, let me reiterate that the fundamental parallels of the story—the widely-acknowledged allegory of The Fall of Man, of sin entering the world through human treachery and God's plan for ultimate sacrifice and resurrection to overcome that fateful event—are not to be dismissed, nor deemed trivial because of their transparency. Particularly for the first-time reader (child or otherwise), these foundational plotlines connect us to that Great Myth which also happens to be true (as Lewis so eloquently articulated, and attributed to Tolkien[†]). The dawning recognition of God's compassion, His love, His justice and His mercy in the face of man's sinfulness is a beautiful and integral—and intentional—component of Lewis' work.

But the allegorical is a tool for Lewis, not the goal. He did not aim to simply retell the salvation story. He intended the reader, I believe, to come away with a more abundant understanding not just of what God's plan for salvation is, but what it means in each of our lives.

[†] See *Tolkien: A Celebration,* edited by Joseph Pearce, p. 184f.

Two Roads through Narnia

For instance, what do we observe in this story about the relationship between a self-sacrificing God and His children? In *The Magician's Nephew*, we were introduced to the Creator Aslan—a Being whose power is equaled only by his compassion for and sorrow over his creation (e.g., a tearful Aslan grieving with Digory over his mother's illness, without disregarding Digory's hand in bringing evil to his new world). In *The Lion, the Witch and the Wardrobe*, we see this powerful Aslan humbly submit himself to Queen Jadis' punishment, again never disregarding Edmund's role in the conflict (yet never belaboring the point, either). Likewise, when Peter takes partial responsibility for Edmund's betrayal, the Great Lion says "nothing either to excuse Peter or to blame him but merely [stands] looking at him with his great golden eyes."[†] Ultimately, we see that Aslan's kindness—not his power nor his wrath—is what leads Edmund back to him (see Romans 2:4). Aslan's unsevered relationship with Edmund offers an honest look at God's overriding love for His broken people: He loved us first, and never stopped (see 1 John 4:19).

Another question: Did you ever wonder while you were reading why the children are so uninquisitive of Aslan? Really—these are naturally curious children who have spent hours exploring this mysterious old house, fascinated by the innumerable rooms and their individual qualities. Their dogged need to know drove them to ask Professor Kirke about Lucy's crazy stories. Yet as the Lion reveals more and more to them about his plan, and about what will come in the future, and about their roles in Narnia, they are silent.

Peter, for one, isn't the least surprised or overwhelmed when Aslan takes him to see the "far-off sight of the castle"[‡] where he will be king. Now, if I were Peter, my mind would have started racing: *Excuse, me, did he say king? But I am only a boy! And just a moment ago I told him I was part to blame for*

[†] C. S. Lewis, *The Lion, the Witch and the Wardrobe*, p. 124.
[‡] Ibid., p. 125.

Edmund's betrayal... How can I be a king? Yet Lewis has Peter say nothing—not a word.

Similarly, the children are mute even in the face of the somewhat odd gifts that are bestowed on them by a rather anachronistic Father Christmas. (Just ask yourself: how can there be Christmas in Narnia without a Christ-child whose birth it would be celebrating? Yet the gifting is essential to the story...) The gifts for Mr. and Mrs. Beaver are reasonable enough—functional tools to help them do what they do best. But the gifts for the children... Not exactly what I would expect under my Christmas tree, Narnian or not.

First, the future King Peter receives a real shield and sword. And even though Father Christmas points out the practicality of the gifts, Peter doesn't ask how to use them, or why he needs them, or in what capacity he may be called upon to apply them. Susan, who receives both offensive and defensive weapons, accepts her gifts so unceremoniously that Lewis does not even describe her response. Then Lucy, whose gift is specifically intended for healing, asserts her bravery but does not question Father Christmas' further explanation that women do not belong in battle. (But what about Susan's bow...)

Other instances of conspicuous speechlessness abound. For example, when Aslan reveals that saving Edmund may be harder than the children imagine, they do not question him. They do not ask what they will do, or what the task will require, or who will be the one most responsible for saving the lost sibling. And Edmund, the guilty betrayer, knows instinctively that as Aslan and Jadis wrestle over his life, silence—not emotional outburst, not desperate plea, not public self-deprecation—is called for. Later, when Aslan, while outlining battle plans with Peter, reveals that he cannot guarantee his presence when the Witch returns, Peter is once again distinctly silent. Then when Aslan acknowledges his loneliness during the trek to the Stone Table (despite the girls' presence), Susan and Lucy do not question him; and when he tells them they can come no further with him, they cry, but say nothing.

Two Roads through Narnia

So what do the Pevensie children demonstrate through their silence? They do not question Aslan—his answer to Jadis' call for blood, his reasons for not allowing them to stay with him in the midst of his anguish, their establishment as Narnian royalty. Edmund does not question the price of his redemption, his forgiveness by Aslan and his siblings or his place as king alongside the others. They weep, they mourn, but they do not question. If all this silence is deliberate on Lewis' part, we have to ask: *what does it mean?*

In my world, I question everything. Like the toddler who learns that magic word *WHY?* and repeats it *ad nauseum*, I am seldom silent when God tells me anything. *Why me? Why this way? What am I supposed to do with this? Are You sure You want me to do this? Isn't there someone more qualified? Have You really forgiven me?* The questions are incessant, and I rarely stop questioning long enough to hear an answer, should He offer one I might want to try to understand.

But the Pevensies, by contrast, instinctively know what it means to trust the Almighty One, and to acknowledge that he knows best regardless of how things appear to be. They know how to accept responsibility as well as redemption, gifts as well as admonition, grace as well as truth: with silence.

And I am brought back to the words of Christ: "I tell you the truth, unless you change and become like little children, you will never enter the kingdom of heaven. Therefore, whoever humbles himself like this child is the greatest in the kingdom of heaven."[†]

So is there more to this story than a repackaging of the gospel in a children's tale? In a word, yes. Much more. More than a casual reading might reveal. More than we might want to admit we missed the first (or twenty-first) time we read the book. More than a theologically-educated mind might wish to find in a "children's" series. More than I could examine in one attempt—and certainly more than I bargained for.

[†] Matthew 18:3-4.

The Horse
and His Boy

Excitement is a wonderful thing when you can feel it building. In May of 2005, while I was rereading *The Horse and His Boy*, the trailer for *The Lion, the Witch and the Wardrobe* made its historic, world-wide debut. And even my TV screen made it plain that the film's vision of Narnia was going to be fairly epic in scope—perhaps even more so than the book from which the film is adapted. The air almost crackled with electricity as my wife and I watched those ninety seconds or so of footage.

Oddly enough, *The Chronicles of Narnia* themselves, in book form, don't really begin to get the epic feel so early in the game. Not until this third chronological story, published fifth of the seven books, does the sweep and scope of C. S. Lewis' vision become so apparent.

Let me explain. Through *The Magician's Nephew*, we of course witness the creation of Narnia; but we also witness the death throes of Charn, are educated about the Wood Between the Worlds, and spend a great deal of time in London. Yes, the book is about Narnia; but it is primarily about Narnia's place in the cosmos. Digory and Polly's story is not just about Narnia.

In a similar way, *The Lion, the Witch and the Wardrobe* introduces us to the character of Narnia and its inhabitants; but three visits are necessary before the story really takes off. And though the Pevensies become High Kings and Queens of Narnia, aging into mature adults there, scant sentences are spent upon that particular part of the story. Instead, the book concludes with yet a third return to our own world.

By contrast, *The Horse and His Boy* begins and ends in Narnia. No narrative framing device distracts us from thorough immersion into the language and culture of the Calormenes. The Pevensie children enter into the story in a perfectly natural fashion—no magic is required for their presence. And for the first time, we feel as though the world of Narnia might really be a place for epic tales: a land we could really inhabit.

As we look at this fine story, Kathy provides a synopsis of the basic plot; Jenn then presents a summary of what makes this particular book so effective and how it amplifies the Narnian vision; and George wraps up with a look at the unique dimension of Aslan that the tale presents.

❧ Once Upon a Time in Calormen ❧

Synopsis by Kathy Bledsoe

On the shore of a country called Calormen lives a very poor fisherman named Arsheesh—and Shasta, a boy who calls him "father." Life is very hard, and it is easier for Arsheesh to find fault with Shasta than to look for things to praise. Curiously, Shasta finds that he has no interest in being an active part of Calormene culture, and is constantly dreaming of whatever might lie in the far North.

One day, a strange man rides in on a fine dappled horse. Arsheesh immediately recognizes that this man is a great lord. This Tarkaan nobleman forces himself upon Arsheesh's hospitality for the night, so Shasta is ousted from the cottage. He sits by a crack in the wall, eavesdropping on the conversation inside. The Tarkaan demands that Arsheesh sell the boy, and in the negotiation process Shasta hears a story that fills him with great delight: Shasta is not Arsheesh's son but an orphan baby rescued from a boat on an incoming tide. At last Shasta understands why he has never been able to feel real love for this man, and why his own fair skin and hair make him so out of place in Calormen.

He goes to the stable (where he will most likely spend the night) and pauses to pet the Tarkaan's beautiful horse. To his great wonderment, the horse speaks to him, and Shasta is introduced to a real Narnian talking horse who was kidnapped as a foal and made a slave to humans in Calormen. He advises Shasta that death would be better than serving in the Tarkaan's house as a slave. The two hatch a plan to escape northward to freedom in Narnia—the horse needing a rider to keep from looking odd by traveling alone, and Shasta needing more than his own two legs to flee with any speed. After setting up a false trail, Shasta and the horse (whose long unpronounceable name gets shortened to "Bree") gallop off into the night.

So begins a journey filled with tales of Bree's exploits as

an enslaved war horse, tales that gradually give way to his longings to forget those days and be a truly free Horse again. They are traveling toward the great city of Tashbaan, the capital of Calormen and the Gateway to the North. One night, Bree and Shasta sense another horse and rider nearby. Bree gallops off inland until the roars of lions force him to change direction several times. The other horse is now galloping beside them and Shasta sees that the rider is quite small and clothed in chain mail. The horses crash and splash across a sea inlet and pause to blow on the other side as one last angry roar draws their attention to a great and terrible lion crouched on the opposite bank. The strange horse speaks, the strange rider tells her to be quiet, and Bree and Shasta discover that the horse, Hwin, is also a Narnian talking horse ridden by a young girl—and that both are also attempting to escape to Narnia. Bree suggests that all four travel together, a suggestion which is roundly approved by Hwin; but animosity between the girl and Shasta threatens to kill the partnership before it begins.

Bree suggests a rest. Aravis Tarkheena, a member of Calormene royalty, tells her story. Here's the gist of it:

Her mother died, and her stepmother hates Aravis (naturally!). Her father promises the young teen in marriage to one Ahoshta Tarkaan who is sixty, humpbacked, and looks like an ape. Aravis prepares to kill herself rather than marry the ape-face—but her horse speaks, preventing the suicide. Aravis and her new-found friend, Hwin, devise a plan to escape for the freedom of Narnia and the North. (Hmmm... Where have we heard that before?) She forces an old and trusted slave to write a letter for her—which she later sends to her father—the contents of which are written as if coming from Ahoshta, saying that he discovered Aravis in the forest and HAD to marry her immediately! This, hopefully, to buy enough time to make good the escape. Ultimately, the two meet up with Bree and Shasta, where our story continues.

The next day, the four move on. They agree to meet at the Tombs of the Ancient Kings on the northern side of Tashbaan if they get separated. On the outskirts of the great city, Shasta and Aravis dirty themselves up and purloin some peasant clothing for Aravis, bundling the horse equipment to look like packs. With admonitions from Bree to go straight through the city, the children join the huge, pressing crowd of humanity that occupies it. They are not even halfway through before Shasta is mistaken by a group of visiting Narnian royalty for Prince Corin of Archenland, a runaway member of their party—and he is whisked away to a palace where he learns that Narnia's Queen Susan is in Tashbaan to become the bride of Prince Rabadash, son of the Tisroc. But Queen Susan has decided that Rabadash is a creep, and yet another escape plan is in the making.

As Shasta listens, he hears of a secret pass across the desert that affords access to Narnia beyond. Shasta also hears of plans to escape aboard the Narnian ship *Splendour Hyaline*, feeling that he cannot possibly reveal who he really is without being punished as a spy. He falls asleep until awakened by a ruckus at the window. The real Corin falls into the room, realizes what has happened with Shasta, and helps Shasta get away, telling him to go to his father, King Lune of Archenland. Returning to the Tombs as agreed, Shasta expects to find his traveling companions, but darkness falls without their arrival. A very large cat appears from nowhere and leads Shasta to the edge of the desert, where it sits facing Narnia. Shasta falls asleep with this cat at his back until awakened by the cries of jackals. Miraculously, the jackals are driven off by a huge lion that Shasta is sure will then eat him. In fear, he clamps his eyes shut, but when nothing happens, he opens them again to see the cat lying once again at his feet. Finally, late the next day, two horses approach... but without Aravis.

Meanwhile... Back in Tashbaan

After watching as Shasta is seized by the Narnians, Aravis is apprehended by an old childhood friend, Tarkheena Lasaraleen, who whisks her away for a visit. Aravis demands that Lasaraleen help her escape and sends Bree and Hwin ahead to the tombs with a servant. As the two girls sneak through the Tisroc's palace, they are forced to hide behind a couch in a room as the Tisroc, the Grand Vizier and Ahoshta himself enter, discussing a plot to invade Narnia, force Queen Susan to marry Rabadash, and extend Calormene rule. Eventually the three leave, and Aravis finally is able to meet her companions at the Tombs. The group then begins the arduous trip across the desert.

Shasta takes the lead, as the one who has heard where a narrow valley is located. The valley gradually widens until they can see the pass that leads from Archenland into Narnia. But Rabadash's army is moving quickly. King Lune must be warned. Another mad gallop is the order of the day. They find even more speed when they are once again chased by a huge, snarling lion. As they run, Shasta notices a great green wall ahead, with an open gate framing a long-bearded man. Looking back, Shasta sees that the lion is almost upon Hwin. He jumps from Bree to go back and help Aravis, but before he can get to her the lion rakes her shoulders with his claws—and departs. The four pound through the gate into a circular enclosure and meet the Hermit of the Southern March, who tells Shasta to run on and warn King Lune. Shasta obeys, leaving the Hermit to care for Aravis and the horses.

Meanwhile... Shasta is running!

Shasta runs right smack into King Lune's hunting party. The King (like the group in the city) also mistakes Shasta for Prince Corin, but Shasta corrects him, quickly explaining that Rabadash and two hundred cavalry are on the way! Shasta is put on a horse to ride with the party to Anvard, but as he has never mastered a regular horse, he soon finds himself separated from the others. A dense fog has descended and Shasta has no idea which way to go. When Rabadash's army comes up behind him, he overhears the plan to lay waste to Archenland. Shasta now realizes that his path to Anvard is blocked; and while he is crying he realizes that someone or something is walking beside him.

This is the great and real meeting between Shasta and Aslan, who explains that he has been with Shasta throughout his journey: forcing him to join with Aravis; comforting and guarding him among the Tombs; giving the horses new incentive to run harder—even long ago pushing a boat carrying a child near death to the shore where a fisherman could find him. Shasta falls at the Lion's feet. Their eyes meet; then Aslan is gone.

As the sun rises, Shasta realizes that he has crossed into Narnia. He quickly meets a talking hedgehog and a rabbit, a Red Dwarf named Duffle and a stag named Chervy who is appointed to take the news of the attack on Anvard to Queen Lucy at Cair Paravel. Later that day, the army of Narnia, led by Lord Peridan and accompanied by King Edmund, Queen Lucy and Prince Corin, begins its journey into battle. Everyone is amazed to see the similarity between Shasta and Corin. The two boys hang back on the end of the column and proceed with the army to Anvard.

Meanwhile... At Anvard's Gates

Rabadash and his army have made a battering ram from a tree and are attempting to break down the gates. The Narnian army arrives and charges down on the Calormenes. Shasta, unsurprisingly, finds himself completely inept in battle.

Meanwhile... Back at the Southern March

The Hermit sits under a beautiful tree and watches the battle reflected in a pool of water, relating what he sees to Bree, Hwin and Aravis. The might of the Narnians—great cats, giants, centaurs, fighting men—prevails over the army of the Calormenes until so many of Rabadash's great warriors are dead or captured that the rest surrender.

Meanwhile... Back at Anvard

Rabadash has managed to get caught on a hook in the wall and is thrashing around like an angry puppet. He is bound and carried into the castle. Corin brings Shasta to King Lune, who astounds Shasta by hugging and kissing him.

Meanwhile... Bree, Aravis and Hwin Meet Aslan

Bree, Aravis and Hwin are interrupted by the arrival of a huge lion leaping over the wall. Bree bolts and must be coaxed back by Aslan; Hwin comes to Aslan readily; and Aravis is told that it was Aslan who wounded her—she learns that her "stripes" are the consequences of her choice to run away and leave her maid to be whipped by her father. As Aslan bounds away back over the hedge, Prince Cor of Archenland is announced—and in walks Shasta to see Aravis!

Shasta and Prince Corin, it turns out, are twins. When they were a few days old, a centaur prophesied that Cor would one day save Archenland. King Lune's chancellor—a spy for the Tisroc—kidnapped Cor, and put to sea with him. By the time the chancellor was captured, Cor and a knight had been set adrift—in the same boat that Aslan had guided to shore for Arsheesh to find. Cor invites Aravis to come and live with King Lune, an invitation which she happily accepts.

Cor, Bree, Aravis and Hwin then travel back to Anvard. Rabadash is brought before the court and proceeds to curse his captors, when suddenly Aslan appears and offers mercy to Rabadash. The Calormene responds by calling Aslan a demon and continuing to revile everyone in sight. Aslan warns the Prince twice before turning him into a donkey, telling him that he will be returned to Tashbaan where he will be restored to human form. However, if he travels more than ten miles from the Temple of Tash, he will turn back into a donkey—finally and forever. Rabadash returns to Tashbaan where the transformation takes place in front of his father's subjects. Rabadash never again goes to war.

There is a great celebration at Anvard. Cor learns that he is heir to the throne of Archenland—which suits Corin (an unwilling future monarch) just fine. Aravis and Cor eventually grow up and marry and become a very good king and queen, as well as the parents of the most famous of all Archenland kings, Ram the Great. Bree and Hwin marry too, though not to each other, and visit Archenland regularly.

And they all live happily ever after.

❧ From a Master Storyteller ❧

Literary Analysis by Jenn Wright

We all know someone for whom storytelling is a craft, a talent carefully honed until we, their very willing audience, are hanging on every word. My brother Rick is one such storyteller. His tales of outdoor adventures never fail to captivate me, and they always promise to send me into hysterics one or two times along the way. His yarns of hunting and hiking exploits with his trusty (albeit stubborn) mule, Louie, are a highlight of family gatherings (for everyone save his wife). I've spent many a spare thought trying to pin down just what makes Rick a great storyteller.

Now, it should be noted that no one else in my immediate family has such a flair for legend-making. Any attempt I might make exceeding a good one-liner, for instance, leaves my audience simply yearning for a conclusion. But Rick has that "special something" down to a fine science—that certain combination of innate talent and practiced technique that draws you into a story as if you were there experiencing the travails with him.

In *The Horse and His Boy*, C. S. Lewis seems to have found that careful equilibrium as well. His myriad writings in both fiction and non-fiction demonstrate his prowess as a powerful writer; yet one can be a skilled writer without being able to tell a decent story. Likewise, one can spin a good yarn and still not have the slightest idea how to relate the story effectively in writing. This is not to say that the first two books (chronologically) in the Narnia series are weak stories or are poorly told—but here Lewis' storytelling abilities and writing skill converge, I believe, to create a fully-fledged tale.

But what makes a well-told story well-told? What transforms a narrative into a legend? In *The Horse and His Boy*, Lewis fleshes out the realm of his stories—and finally the world of Narnia becomes one into which the reader can fully enter.

Setting

One foundational strength of this segment of the chronicles is that there is a strong sense of place, something which is less well-defined in the first two installments. In both *The Magician's Nephew* and *The Lion, the Witch and the Wardrobe*, there is some unsettled-ness over the coming and going between worlds. Since no single world—not just "place," but entire world—is "The Setting" of the first two books, the audience may feel somewhat ungrounded, perhaps even uneasy. In *The Horse and His Boy*, not only do we have single place to call The Setting, but we have a sense of geography, of the lay of the land. We see how different areas of this world interact, and we travel with Shasta and his cohorts through numerous climates, cultures and countries, on the way to The Great Land of Narnia itself. Knowing exactly where we are, where we have come from, and where we are headed allows us to become more fully absorbed in the other details of the travels.

Language

While written stories and oral accounts have their differences in language (one rarely speaks in the same style as one writes), language is the basis of a story. One doesn't use poetic language and flowery descriptions in a calculus text; neither are sunsets or a lover's eyes frequently expressed in mathematical terminology. Instead, we use specific language styles to communicate our purposes most effectively; English words and grammar may serve both expository and descriptive purposes, but the language used is almost invariably different. Thus, with storytelling (both written and spoken), a look at the use of language sheds light on the art itself.

In *The Horse and His Boy*, Lewis delights us with a perfect example of both written and oral storytelling. While his own skill in descriptive narration is evident throughout the book, he also offers unusual insight into oral storytelling by dedicating an entire chapter ("At the Gates of Tashbaan") to Aravis'

Two Roads through Narnia

introduction of herself in expert oral-tradition style. Her life to this point becomes the story.

In a similar way, Lewis' storycrafting takes a rather poetic turn in this book—poetic language takes a more prominent role in his descriptions of the people, the lands, the animals. More than either *The Magician's Nephew* or *The Lion, the Witch and the Wardrobe*, we are left with vivid mental images of *The Horse and His Boy*. We can smell the dirty fishiness of southern Calormen. We can picture old Arsheesh wheedling and conniving as he and the Tarkaan stranger haggle over the price for poor Shasta. We feel the warmth of the oversized cat against Shasta's back among the tombs. The travels through the desert leave us slightly thirsty. Lewis' skilled descriptions play on all five senses, with heat "shivering" up in waves from the sand, and the Lion "tearing" Aravis' shoulders; and the experience becomes that much more real for us, his captive audience.

Not to be overlooked, the issue of language itself has bearing. In Calormen, we find Calormene terms—Tarkaan, Tarkheena, Tisroc, just to mention a few—that convey a sense of foreignness unknown thus far in the Narnian Chronicles. In Narnia itself, everyone spoke the King's English—for all we knew the characters were white Anglo-Saxons, and people as well as talking animals spoke modern-day British English. Even Jadis, though from the world of Charn, experienced no language barrier (though the cultural barrier was certainly evident). Yet in Calormen, there are indications of racial differences (southern vs. northern, dark and light skin, etc.), and the Calormene vocabulary emphasizes a sense of the exotic—the introduction of a truly "new" place in which we are aliens.

Characters

Yet another strength of *The Horse and His Boy* is the development of characters into people (and animals) with whom we can identify. Though *The Magician's Nephew* and *The Lion, the Witch and the Wardrobe* all have numerous good and evil and

60

somewhere-in-between characters, when reading *The Horse and His Boy* we find ourselves empathizing with the characters more than in the previous novels. It is easy to share Shasta's shame upon his first confrontations with the somewhat haughty and proud Aravis, who seems to put on airs and condescend to the poor boy. In the dark night of waiting at the tombs, we can feel Shasta's fear creep in as the light fades. The horrible dread is nearly palpable when Aravis and her irritatingly self-absorbed friend Lasaraleen are breathlessly hiding in the same room as the secret council of the Tisroc, the Grand Vizier and Aravis' betrothed, Ahoshta Tarkaan. Even these three men, though only occupying a small part of the story, leave a lasting impression— perhaps more so than even Jadis in *The Magician's Nephew*, for all her hateful behaviors. And, of course, what child has not hoped—even slightly believed, at some point—that he, like Shasta, is a long-lost prince, just waiting to be found by his royal family?

Such empathetic characters draw us into the story until we are a substantive part of it—breathing quietly with Aravis during the secret council, so as not to be heard by the illustrious men; jumping ever so slightly when the Lion's claws rake across the girl's back; laughing in spite of ourselves at the humiliation of Rabadash. Such things are evidence of our incorporation into the story, a direct outgrowth of our connections with the characters.

Foreshadowing

We would be quite mistaken, I believe, to address Lewis' art of storytelling in *The Horse and His Boy* without giving adequate attention to foreshadowing. While it can be overused and oversimplified (and some might argue that Lewis' use of foreshadowing is a bit heavy-handed in this case), the technique does draw the audience into the story by hinting at what is to come. From the first page of *The Horse and His Boy*, we know that Shasta's current living situation is not as it might appear. Arsheesh is described as a man whom Shasta *calls* father, not as

Shasta's father. Moreover, just a few lines later, much is made of Shasta's "Northern" likeness—rather fair-skinned and light-haired, unlike the southern Calormene "darkness of cheek." So from the very beginning of the story we are engaged and enticed, wondering what Shasta's past and future have in common. And when, near the end of the tale, Cor's true identity is revealed, we are at once happy for him and happy for ourselves—for we have grown to genuinely like Shasta/Cor, and his good fortune serves the audience as well.

So what makes this story a good story well-told? I suppose I could try to use mathematical terminology and root-cause analysis to offer some sort of explanation. Above, I've noted some specific literary strengths which certainly contribute to the success of a story's telling, but I would be hard-pressed to think that I have in some way uncovered that certain aspect of storytelling that keeps us wide-eyed and open-eared and glued to our seats. Rather, I think I have merely rediscovered that—mathematically—a good story well-told is more than a sum of all its literarily skilled and crafted parts.

❧ The Narnia Trinity ☙

Spiritual Commentary by George Rosok

After reading the first three books of the C. S. Lewis' Narnia series, I can't help thinking of them as a special kind of trilogy: a trinity—an illustration of the Holy Trinity, in fact.

The Magician's Nephew introduced Aslan as the Creator. We first saw him singing Narnia into existence. With his song the day, night, land, water, plants and animals were brought to life. He determined who would rule in this land, and he knew its future.

In *The Lion, the Witch and the Wardrobe,* he more clearly represented Christ, the Son. He saved Edmund from his sins of treachery and saved all of Narnia by allowing himself to be sacrificed on the Stone Table by the White Witch and her minions. After being watched over by Susan and Lucy throughout the night, at sunup he was gone. He then reappeared and presented himself to Susan and Lucy, and though they feared he may have been a ghost, he was most certainly alive. He and his believers went on to overcome and destroy the witch and her evil army. (Lewis also made it plain in this volume that Aslan is but the son of the Emperor-Beyond-the-Sea.)

In *The Horse and His Boy,* Aslan's role changes again and models the function of the Holy Spirit. His activities are often in the background. The story's characters—and often the readers—do not know what Aslan's purposes are. He appears as early as the second chapter but we are not aware that it is Aslan until much later. Usually he comes in some unexpected form and does something that seems unrelated or perhaps even harmful to the characters. It is as though he is ever-present, always knowing, but seldom in a form that is understood or recognizable to the participants of the events. This "guiding spirit" aspect of Aslan's character—the third manifestation of the Godhead in the Trinity—warrants further discussion.

In chapter two, Bree—the Narnian horse who has helped the young protagonist, Shasta, escape from Calormen—hears what he believes is another horse and rider. He devises a plan to avoid them, but before he can execute it a ferocious lion chases them. Then another lion appears to be chasing the other party. Against their plans and wishes Bree, Shasta and the other travelers—Hwin, another Narnian horse, and Aravis, a young Calormene girl escaping an arranged marriage—are forced together. They decide to form an alliance—a decision that will ensure that together they will reach Archenland in spite of separations and many trials along the way.

At the time they think it is only chance that has brought them together; but this is just the first of many times in the story that Aslan intervenes in order to direct events. Their perception is that they have been attacked by lions, not that they are being divinely led. Aslan even appears to be two lions, to chase the two pairs together.

Aslan appears in other forms as well. When Shasta becomes separated from the rest of the group in Tashbaan, he makes his way out of the city to the group's pre-determined meeting place—the Tombs on the edge of the desert. Here Shasta is frightened and alone. He goes to the desert side of the tombs to wait for the rest of the group, but it is a very lonely and frightening place—the vast desert ahead, the ghostly tombs behind. A large cat appears and this familiar-looking animal provides comfort and company in the lonely night. Although the cat is not overly friendly, he provides a warm back for Shasta to lean against.

Later, approaching jackals waken the sleeping Shasta. Suddenly a huge animal appears and scares them off. Shasta is afraid that it is another lion and that it will eat him, but then recognizes that it is only the same large cat. In this case, Shasta, although frightened, doesn't know what the jackals are or the danger they present, nor does he know that it is Aslan who appears as the cat to repel the threat. Another point of faith: dangers aren't always fully perceived, nor are blessings—in this case the blessing of Aslan the Comforter.

Aravis also has lessons to learn, and one of these is to overcome the arrogance and lack of compassion engendered by being raised in a privileged and extravagantly wealthy environment. Slavery and ill treatment of others who are considered inferior are common and expected patterns in her world. In order to make her escape from her father (and an arranged marriage), she drugs the servant girl assigned to her by her stepmother. Aravis coolly states that the girl was probably beaten for sleeping late, but it's okay because she was a tool and a spy of her stepmother. "I am very glad they should beat her,"[†] is Aravis' comment to her companions.

This haughty attitude is brought down later in the book when another lion attacks them as they hurry through Archenland. The lion chases Aravis and Hwin and brutally claws Aravis' back. Again, this is Aslan directing events. Later, when Aravis finally meets Aslan, he explains that it was he who tore her back so that the wounds would match those received by the servant girl. "The scratches on your back, tear for tear, throb for throb, blood for blood, were equal to the stripes laid on the back of your stepmother's slave." He did this because Aravis "needed to know what it felt like."[‡] Through this lesson, although harsh and painful, she does understand the consequences of the pain caused by her presumptuous and haughty actions.

Although Aravis' cause to escape her father was justifiable—and the servant girl may indeed have been a spy—it was wrong to let someone else suffer because of her own actions, and even worse to feel no remorse. By shaping events not understood at the time, Aslan helps Aravis to recognize her arrogant attitude, and she learns humility and compassion.

Bree also benefits from Aslan's teaching. Because he is a talking horse from Narnia and has also served as the steed of a Calormene officer participating in many battles, he is likewise

[†] C. S. Lewis, *The Horse and His Boy*, p. 40.
[‡] Ibid., p. 194.

arrogant, and often heedless of both danger and the needs of others. Shortly after the four join together, they must contrive a plan to get through Tashbaan undetected. Shasta suggests they use disguises. Hwin adds that they might be less likely to be detected if they went directly through the city, because they would draw less attention in a crowd. She suggests that the children dress in rags and pretend to drive the horses so people will think she and Bree are packhorses. Aravis says this is ridiculous because no one would believe Bree was anything but a war horse. Bree haughtily agrees, but in the end it is Shasta and Hwin's plan that is employed.

Bree also puts the party at risk when he says they should all take time to sleep after traveling through the desert and into the canyon approaching Archenland. Compounding the problem, even though they oversleep, he insists that they eat before moving on because he thinks they must be ahead of Rabadash's army. Bree's rationalized self-centeredness nearly costs them the advantage of their lead over Rabadash. When they do realize how close Rabadash is and they are racing for Archenland, Aslan appears again as the ferocious lion and attacks them, going after Aravis in particular. When she is wounded, it is the boy, Shasta, who courageously goes back to try to help her while Bree runs for his life. Realizing this, Bree is brought low; but he learns humility and will be a better creature for it.

But the race to Archenland isn't just about Bree's pride. Although all four travelers (and Bree in particular) are certain they are absolutely exhausted, they find additional reserves when they believe they are under attack. Aslan guides the party's members to reach inside themselves in order to persevere and overcome the trial at hand. Throughout the story, events occur which make the way difficult and dangerous. It is through these trials that all of the travelers mature, becoming stronger, wiser and more humble.

Shasta also has lessons to learn. In chapter eleven, Shasta goes ahead to find King Lune of Archenland and him warn him that Rabadash is coming to attack his kingdom. It would appear that Shasta has done his duty and will be safe with King Lune's party. But as they travel, Shasta and the ordinary horse provided by King Lune cannot keep up with the King's party. Shasta is not a real horseman and is lost in the fog. Aslan once again appears— a bodiless voice in the fog—but though unseen, he is protecting Shasta by preventing Shasta and his horse from riding off the trail and over a cliff.

Aslan later reveals himself to Shasta, but only upon being invited. When Shasta asks who he is, Aslan replies in a fashion that is like a trinity itself: Three times, he responds, "Myself." The scene is reminiscent of God's response when Moses asks what he should say to the Israelites when they ask who has sent him. God tells Moses, "This is what you are to say to the Israelites: 'I AM has sent me to you.'"[†]

Once invited, Aslan the Guide and Comforter assures Shasta that he is real even when he cannot be seen, and he coaxes Shasta, "Tell me your sorrows."[‡] Shasta tells him all of the hardship in his life, including not having a mother and father and growing up with the stern, insensitive fisherman in Calormen. He tells Aslan about his escape and all the trials he and his companions have been through until that moment. Finally, Aslan reveals that he was there all along. He was the "two lions" that brought the two separate parties together. He was the cat at the tombs. He was the one who chased them and gave the horses new strength to outrun Rabadash.

He was even the one who, when Shasta was a child, pushed the boat he was lying in to shore so it would be found by the fisherman.

What's more—and though Shasta does not realize it until morning—Aslan helps guide Shasta into Narnia while they are talking. Shasta meets several of the creatures living there and a couple of them have the good sense to notify the royalty at Cair Paravel so they can come to the aid of King Lune of Archenland.

[†] Exodus 3:14.

[‡] C. S. Lewis, *The Horse and His Boy*, p. 157.

Also, it is here that Shasta is fed and restored. He is able to march back to Archenland with this army from Narnia, accompanied by Prince Corin—who is revealed to be Shasta's twin.

Aslan also appears in Archenland after the battle is won. Through all his direct and indirect participation, a prophecy is fulfilled: Shasta, who is actually Prince Cor of Archenland, has returned to save Archenland in its most needful hour.

And here we find that not everyone is prepared to be guided by Aslan's influence. The Lion offers mercy to Rabadash, who has been captured, but Rabadash, ever the arrogant disbeliever, refuses it and even attempts to frighten Aslan and the others at his "trial." Aslan warns him to accept the offer, but Rabadash will have none of it, so Aslan turns him into a donkey. Even then he grants Rabadash some degree of mercy, explaining to him that he can become human again if he goes to the temple of Tash and stands before the altar at the great Autumn Feast. Once returned to human form he will remain human only if he does not travel more than ten miles from the temple. If he does, he will be turned back into a donkey—*permanently*. Consequently, once Rabadash eventually becomes ruler of Calormen, he does not wage war because he cannot leave to fight, and he fears that his army will turn on him if, while fighting abroad, he is not there to direct it.

So what we find in *The Horse and His Boy* is a remarkable illustration of how God's Spirit moves in our own lives. While most of the story seems initiated by the principal characters, the events are always changed and governed by Aslan. Eventually, all things work out according to his plan and to the benefit of those who grow by his direction.

How many times in life must we also have faith that certain things happen for a purpose, all evidence to the contrary—just as the Bible tells us? Often we must extend our faith, must be reminded that we may never know exactly why things happen.

In this story, Shasta is fortunate enough to find out what Aslan has done, and to discover his own role in Aslan's plans. But most of us are still in the middle of our own stories. We must take it on faith that the events of our life have taken place for a reason;

and we must rely on that faith in the worst times of our life—even if we never know or understand the purpose of what has happened.

Prince
Caspian

With *Prince Caspian*, C. S. Lewis ventures farther into the broader world of Narnia. Now, it's certainly true that we visited Calormen in *The Horse and His Boy*—so learning in this book that Telmar, the land from which Caspian's people once hailed, is yet another of Narnia's neighbors is perhaps no great surprise. But some nagging questions about the human population of this world are answered. After all, if every Narnian human is descended from King Frank and Queen Helen, whom we met in *The Magician's Nephew*, who are the Calormenes and Telmarines? Where did *they* come from?

But in this tale, the world of Narnia becomes broader not just due to genealogy and geography. It also grows because the lines between the White Hats and Black Hats becomes just a little fuzzier. Yes, the plot of *The Lion, the Witch and the Wardrobe* turned on Edmund's selfish treachery; and Digory, Aravis and others in the Chronicles have also been less than perfectly motivated and behaved. But the narration of the previous tales, at least, has made it perfectly clear who the heroes and villains of those stories were.

In Prince Caspian, though, the roles that the characters play are a bit more complicated. The titular hero of the story, it turns out, is really the most chief of those we would naturally assume are the Black Hats; and, unlike with Shasta in *The Horse and His Boy*, this time it's not a case of mistaken identity. Caspian really is a Telmarine. Further, more than just one of the folks in the camp of the White Hats turns out to be a villain. So, in a twisted but realistic fashion, and in more ways than one, Narnia starts looking more and more like our own world.

For our treatment of this volume, Jenn and I offer a lightly tongue-in-cheek story synopsis intended as a nod to the story structure of *Prince Caspian* itself. George then bravely critiques the novel against the very standards that Lewis himself set for the genre of "children's stories." Also, Kathy takes a look at the spiritual significance of yet another (seemingly) warped aspect of the story: Aslan's "holiday" with Bacchus and the boys—and girls!

❧ Tales within Tales ❧

Synopsis by Greg and Jenn Wright

What child, while waiting for the bus to take him to school, hasn't wished to be whisked away to world without exams and bullies and teachers lurking over your shoulder? Well, Peter, Susan, Edmund and Lucy have just experienced this very thing. And Jenn is here to tell you what happens to them when they are pulled from the local train station back into Narnia...

Like any siblings, each blames the others for the tugging that eventually deposits them in a different world. But everyone happily agrees that exploration takes precedence over arithmetic and penmanship. Following the sound of water, they soon find a beautiful beach, and, shoeless, walk the shore until they find fresh water. They discover that they are trapped on an island. After eating lunch, the quartet heads into the woods to explore, and much to their delight they stumble upon an apple orchard near the ruins of a castle.

Exploring the ruins, they notice that they are somewhat familiar with the layout of the castle. When Susan finds a ruby-eyed chess piece, it is clear: they have been brought back to Narnia, and are exploring the ruins of their own palace, Cair Paravel. They locate their treasure house to retrieve the gifts that Aslan once gave them—but Susan's horn, which promises instant help with a single blow, is nowhere to be found.

After a restless night, the children try to find a way off of the island. They notice a boat just off shore with three people in it; two tall figures appear to be trying to wrestle a third shorter person into the water. Susan takes up her bow and shoots, hitting one of the tall men in the helmet and knocking him overboard. The second tall man dives overboard, leaving the tied-up third figure alone in the boat. The children swim out to the boat and pull it in, curious to hear the story of the rescued little man.

And I'm tired now, so Greg can tell you the story of Trumpkin the dwarf...

Right. You see, Narnia is no longer the happy-go-lucky place it was under the Pevensie Kings and Queens. It's ruled now by the Telmarines who, contrary to the way their name sounds, have nothing to do with the sea. In fact, they hate it. In fact, they hate just about everything that Narnia ever stood for.

Anyway, the rightful Telmarine heir to the throne of Narnia, orphaned young Prince Caspian, is being taken advantage of by his ruthless uncle, King Miraz. This despot conspires to persecute and repress the "Old Narnians." At the real top of his agenda is making sure that his own illegitimate line stays on the throne. Fortunately for Prince Caspian, Uncle Miraz has made the mistake of handing his nephew's education over to a deep-cover Old Narnian, a half-dwarf named Doctor Cornelius. This wise old boy fills Caspian in on the truth of things in Narnia, and has enough of his wits about him to spirit Caspian away when Miraz is lucky enough to sire a son.

Caspian flees, taking with him the famous magical horn that the Doc gave him. Yes: the horn that Susan left behind somehow those many centuries ago when the very High Kings and Queens tumbled back through the wardrobe. You know.

As luck would have it, I guess, Caspian's horse dashes him against a branch, knocking him out cold and leaving him to be found by a troupe of Old Narnians that includes the badger Trufflehunter and two dwarfs: the grumpy Nikabrik and our friend Trumpkin. They fill him in on the incipient rebellion of the Old Narnians. And in Caspian, they think they've found a leader—or at least a figurehead. Under the influence of Reepicheep the very feisty mouse and a handful of other insurgents (including Doctor Cornelius, who joins the gang), Caspian agrees to lead an open rebellion against King Miraz.

They dash off to Aslan's How, a sacred tunnel-riddled earthwork mound that houses the broken stone table upon which Aslan was sacrificed to save Narnia oh-so-long-ago. Miraz is right on their heels, of course, with a real Telmarine army, and things do not go so well for Caspian and his host. Caspian agrees that the only course of action is to use the magical horn to summon help—help of an indeterminate nature, arriving Aslan-only-knows where. They must cover three possible sacred sites: Aslan's How itself, Lantern Waste, and Cair Paravel. Trumpkin draws the assignment for latter site, and as he sets off through the woods he hears the call of the horn. He's not particularly sure it'll do any good, but it sounds impressive enough.

But Trumpkin is waylaid by some loyalists to Miraz, and the louts decide to take him to the dreaded ghost-laden coasts and send him to his death in a few feet of nasty seawater. Of course, they end up bringing him with haste, and in good time, right into the arms of the waiting children. As we have seen.

And now, it is time for another tale. Back to you, Jenn...

Trumpkin complains that the horn brought none of the promised help. After weapons challenges with Susan and Edmund, however, and a healing drop of Lucy's ointment to a shoulder wound, Trumpkin is convinced that the quartet is the Royal article. The five set off in the boat toward the upper reaches of Glasswater Creek. From there, they will take to the woods until they come upon the Great River, and ultimately Aslan's How and King Caspian himself.

Lucy, being the only one not subject to the hard physical labor of rowing, cannot sleep that night. A short distance from camp, she calls out to the trees to awaken them; and indeed there is a gentle rustling. In the morning, the group begins the hike toward the Great River in earnest. When they come to a precipice, Peter laments that this could not be the valley of the Rush, a tributary of the Great River. Trumpkin, however, reminds Peter that it has been hundreds of years, and the landscape is bound to have changed dramatically since the children were last here. While Peter and Trumpkin are talking, Lucy looks up and sees none other than the Great Lion himself. She instantly understands where they should go. Excitedly, she points out Aslan to the others—who do not see him, and do not believe that she did, either. However, Lucy persists, explaining to them that Aslan wants them to go up, not down, as Peter and Trumpkin have decided to do. Still unconvinced, they take a vote, and the party heads down. Lucy follows bitterly.

The slope down the Rush gets more steep and dangerous. Just when they look up and see the Great River, renewing their hope of joining King Caspian in time for battle, they are ambushed. It becomes abundantly clear that Lucy had been right. They turn around to head back up the steep rocky slope they just hazarded down, and take to the high ground instead.

At camp that night, exhaustion pulls everyone into a deep sleep almost immediately. Lucy, however, is awakened from her slumber by hearing someone calling her name. She crawls from her makeshift bed to witness the movement of the trees. Making her way through them, she finds Aslan waiting for her. She runs to him. In their embrace, he chastises her for her complicity in going down into the gorge with the others, instead of following his directions to go up. Lucy tries to blame her failure to follow on the others—but Aslan reiterates his desire for her obedience. He instructs her to wake the others, tell them of his presence, and lead the others by following him, whether they do or not.

This time, Lucy obeys. This time, the others comply (Susan rather noisily) and begin the day's journey. Soon Edmund catches a glimpse of Aslan's shadow, and Peter quickly follows suit. After climbing up the opposite bank, they find themselves in view of Aslan's How—with the Great Lion standing resplendently in full view. Each of them (including Susan, finally) approach Aslan. True to his nature, Aslan forgives them, then addresses Trumpkin, who is scared witless of the giant feline. Fortunately, the dwarf moves toward Aslan and their friendship is playfully sealed.

As dawn breaks, Aslan sends the boys and the dwarf to the field to await battle; Susan and Lucy are left to watch. Suddenly the Great Lion tilts his gloriously maned head back and roars with a force unlike anything ever heard. Susan and Lucy see movement where there had been stillness before, as the trees come out around Aslan. Other creatures join the joyous dance before the battle—a scene which Greg will relate...

Well, the real complicating factor at this point is that Nikabrik has brought in some rather unsavory characters to advise Caspian. From the besieged Old Narnian perspective, help has not come; the call has gone unanswered. So the ever-sour Nikabrik brings a Hag and a Werewolf to Aslan's How in an attempt to summon dark powers to Caspian's aid—the spirit of the White Witch, in fact. Naturally, this suggestion doesn't sit too well with Aslan's faithful. Just as Nikabrik's, um, "friends" are about to force themselves on Caspian, Peter, Edmund and Trumpkin slay the malcontent traitors. Prince Caspian has narrowly avoided an enormous disaster.

In an effort to buy time for whatever Aslan has in store, Peter dashes off a challenge of single combat to King Miraz, who is disingenuously manipulated into accepting by a pair of ambitious lords. A truce is declared and the armies convene to watch the two kings match each other in a contest of arms.

In the early going, Peter fares well against Miraz. In spite of his surprising showing, however, he injures one of his wrists and is unable to properly use his shield. Fortunately, a rest break is called and Peter is able to find a makeshift solution to allow him to continue. He again does well, pressing Miraz hard. After landing a near-fatal glancing blow, the Telmarine stumbles—and his conspiratorial lords jump at the opportunity to slay him while he is down, trying to make it seem as if they are coming to his aid. Bedlam ensues and battle is joined.

It does not go well for the Telmarines, for Caspian's weakened army is now joined by vast numbers of tree-spirits. The horn has now been fully answered. Aslan, the Pevensie children and the full force of Old Narnia have all been roused. The Telmarine army is in full retreat, only to find its route of escape destroyed.

While Peter and Caspian have been managing the front, Aslan—with the girls, Bacchus and a host of others in tow—has been working in the rear to conduct a massive party of deconstruction. The entire Telmarine infrastructure has been pulled down behind the army in a chaotic yet purposefully joyous procession. The army has no choice but to surrender.

Though he feels wholly inadequate to the task—a prerequisite for the job, says Aslan—Caspian assumes leadership of Narnia as its king. Lucy uses her diamond vial, that ancient gift from Aslan, to revive Reepicheep, and Aslan restores his severed tail. Many knighthoods are bestowed, the surviving Telmarines are made captive in Beruna, and the victorious host of Old Narnians settles in for a wild and glorious celebration.

The next day, Aslan issues an ultimatum to the defeated Telmarines: if they are unable or unwilling to submit themselves gladly to the authority of King Caspian, they will be provided with a new home if they present themselves to Aslan. Those who come to avail themselves of this unique mercy discover an amazing fact. Aslan tells them that they are native to neither Narnia nor Telmar, and will be sent back to the place from whence they originally came: a remote desert island in this, our very own world! Aslan constructs a portal to our world, and the Telmarines find their way home after many long centuries.

Following them, not far behind but bound for a far different destination, are Peter, Susan, Edmund and Lucy. They find themselves once again back at the train station where their strange journey started, older for a while and now younger again, but still a little wiser and more mature. Peter and Susan will never visit Narnia again.

❧ Short of the Standard ❧

Literary Analysis by George Rosok

In his essay "On Three Ways of Writing for Children," C. S. Lewis suggests that the only reason you should write a children's story is if the "children's story is the best art-form for something you have to say."[†] When reading the stories in the Narnia series, I sometimes try to put myself in the place of a child who is reading the story for the first time. I find it necessary because at times in these stories the allegory seems too obvious or a plot line comes off as too contrived; and, I think, as an adult reader I may be a bit jaded.

Perhaps an inexperienced reader—a child—would not have the same opinion. A child might enjoy sorting out the convolutions of certain story lines or thrill at explicitly associating a situation in the story to an incident in "real" life. In discussing these stories, one of my friends commented how important and powerful discovering and understanding stories on that level can be for a young reader. But Lewis states in the same essay that he is "almost inclined to set it up as canon that a children's story which is enjoyed only by children is a bad story."[‡] Given this assertion and also the importance of the child's process of discovery, I'm sorry to say that *Prince Caspian* seems to fail Lewis' own test. What happens in the story is too often based on coincidence and convenience. Characters move and act not by a well-developed sequence of events but more because Lewis is able to conveniently explain something that has taken or is about to take place.

Before I go too far down the road describing what bothers me about this story, I want to mention the parts that I did enjoy, particularly the characters and the setting. Trumpkin's

---

[†] C. S. Lewis, "On Three Ways of Writing for Children," *Of Other Worlds*, p. 23.
[‡] Ibid., p. 24.

storytelling, for instance, satisfyingly brought the entire story up to date (if it failed to explain how he came to be with the children in the first place—but more on that later). The main characters, Peter, Susan, Edmund and Lucy, whom we first met in *The Lion, the Witch and the Wardrobe*, are people that we all can relate to. Through their adventures they have acquired admirable amounts of bravery, honesty and intelligence, but as people, moreover young people, they can also be stubborn, cranky and impulsive. I enjoyed watching Lucy, in spite of her uncertainty and reluctance to contradict her older siblings, determine to follow Aslan—as he says she must do even if it means she must leave them.

I also enjoyed the wise Doctor Cornelius; his animal counterpart the badger, Trufflehunter; the practical Trumpkin; the friendly Bulgy Bears; the slow-witted giant, Wimbleweather; and the overly compensating mouse, Reepicheep (although I hate his name!). Even the villains—such as Nikabrik, King Miraz and his plotting lords—are interesting to watch and listen to. And all are placed in the woods, castles, rivers, hills and meadows of Narnia, which Lewis does a wonderful job of describing.

But then these characters are required to participate in the action. While most of the ordinary occurrences (and many of the not-so-ordinary) are logical, and I can follow them without overtly slapping my forehead, it only takes a few instances of foggy logic and contrivance for the story to run off its rails. One such example, as mentioned above, is the appearance of Trumpkin at the island where the children find themselves after being magically yanked away from a British train station. Though I enjoy his bit of storytelling after they rescue him, even in that are seeds of convenient occurrences that weigh on the story later; and when I come to find out the coincidences that had to occur in order for him to meet the children at the island, I only wish his story could have continued on in some other direction. Alas, on we go anyway.

In chapter five, Caspian's aunt, Queen Prunaprismia, seems ill—but it turns out she is actually about to give birth. When a boy is born, Caspian's life is suddenly in danger because he is no longer needed by his uncle, King Miraz, to succeed the throne. This pregnancy is a cheap surprise sprung on the reader. Isn't Caspian old enough and smart enough to have noticed that the Queen was pregnant? Wouldn't wise Doctor Cornelius, who must have known she was pregnant, have previously considered that a male heir might be produced? He would have immediately known the danger to Caspian and would have had months to prepare and plan for that eventuality. Instead, at the birth of the Miraz's son, Doctor Cornelius tells Caspian he must flee for his life in the middle of the night—also dropping the bombshell that Caspian is the true King of Narnia. Doctor Cornelius explains that Miraz murdered his brother, Caspian's father, the previous King Caspian of Narnia. (I also find it curious that King Miraz's son is never mentioned again. Though it turns out Caspian is the rightful king and Miraz is dealt with, I think the Queen and their son merit some mention in order to tie off that loose end.)

Before Caspian leaves, Doctor Cornelius gives him Susan's Magic Horn. This is foreshadowed earlier in the book when the children discover it missing from the treasure room at the now ancient, island-bound castle of Cair Paravel. Doctor Cornelius has oh-so-conveniently acquired it by enduring terrors and uttering spells because it just so happens that Caspian will need it later in order to summon the children into Narnia and into the story. Perhaps if Lewis had given more time to explain how Cornelius would come into possession of such an important talisman (and plot device) it would make more of the rest of the story easier to believe; instead, it is just one of several rabbits he pulls out of a hat.

After Caspian flees to the mountains to the south, on the slopes of Archenland he meets and helps organize the true citizens of Narnia—the dwarfs, talking animals and mythic creatures who have fled and gone into hiding. With the counsel of the centaur, Glenstorm, they determine that they must go to war. In a short couple of paragraphs (and without much trouble or muster) they move to Aslan's How and are soon engaged with Miraz's troops; and these battles go badly. This quickly brings us to one of the main aspects of the plot that bothers me—how Trumpkin and the children come to meet at Cair Paravel.

A council decides that Caspian will blow Susan's horn in the hope that Aslan or the fabled Kings Peter and Edmund and Queens Susan and Lucy will come to help them defeat Miraz's army. Trumpkin is sent to the coast in case help arrives there. At this point we know what happens when he gets there: he is captured and then rescued by the children. But in order for him to get captured he had to do something that even Lewis (by way of Trumpkin himself) has to explain and apologize for. The practical and careful dwarf says, "As if I'd no more sense than a giant, I risked a short cut across open country to cut off a big loop of the river, and was caught." Trumpkin adds, "Anyone else would have run me through there and then."[†]

But Trumpkin has been "fortunate" enough to be caught by one of Miraz's lords, a "pompous fool" who intends a grand execution by sending Trumpkin "down 'to the ghosts' in the full ceremonial way."[‡] He is placed in a boat with two of the lord's soldiers who are interrupted in their mission to drown the dwarf by Susan's well-aimed arrows. So by this series of convenient events Trumpkin is able to meet Peter, Susan, Edmund and Lucy, and the saving of Narnia and the rest of the story is able to proceed. But why is this pompous lord off in the wild in the first place, instead of helping engage Caspian's army? Why, in the heat of a pitched battle, can two soldiers be spared for days, disposing of a spy in such a convoluted way? Why the ceremonious effort? Ah, because Trumpkin needs to "meet cute" with the children.

The children and Trumpkin eventually meet up with Aslan, as well as Silenus, Bacchus and the Maenads—"his fierce, madcap girls"[§]—and together they find their way to Aslan's How. Peter challenges King Miraz to single combat to avoid risking further bloodying of Caspian's army. By the treachery of a couple

---

[†] C. S. Lewis, *Prince Caspian*, p. 95.
[‡] Ibid.
[§] Ibid, p. 192.

of Miraz's own lords, Miraz is defeated and killed. By the help of the awakened trees of the Narnian Woods, the Telmarine army is routed and run off to Beruna where the Telmarines hope to make their escape over the bridge that now spans the ford. But the bridge is gone, so they surrender.

Here begins one of the most curious scenes in the book, where Lewis explains the convenient necessity of the missing bridge. While Lewis likely has his purposes for this scene, and it may be important to his overall purpose for this story and for its place in the Narnia series, from a purely literary standpoint it feels like he opens the back door of the whole production and moves it to the burlesque theater next door.

And so the narrator starts the explanation by rightly asking, "But what had happened to the bridge?"[†] Silenus, Bacchus and the Maenads are still with Aslan, Susan and Lucy. The girls wake up and Aslan tells them they will make a holiday. Everyone is up laughing and playing instruments. The girls climb onto Aslan and they are off. With the help of Bacchus' magic vines the bridge is pulled down—but why?—and the revelers wade across the river and into the town. They scare away a shrewish schoolmarm and most of her class except one girl, Gwendolyn, who joins them. Then the Maenads help her "take off some of the unnecessary and uncomfortable clothes that she was wearing."[‡] From there on through the rest of the chapter, the party winds through the nearby countryside scaring off most people, but they are joined by various animals and a few free-spirited locals. Except for taking down the bridge, little of this seems to have much to do with the story. It feels like a superfluous song and dance number in a staged musical. Eventually the revelers find their way to where Miraz's army is being held at bay by Peter's victorious army.

Following this party (and then another to celebrate the victory), Aslan is prepared to grant the Telmarines mercy. And it

[†] C. S. Lewis, *Prince Caspian*, p. 191.
[‡] Ibid., p. 195.

is here in one long paragraph that Lewis, through Aslan, strings together a number of wild coincidences that explain how the Telmarines came to be in Narnia. They are descended from pirates from Earth. These pirates were shipwrecked on an island. Several of the pirates and their women fled from the others to a mountain where they discovered a cave. In the cave was a magical place that connected Earth and the world of Narnia. They were transported to Telmar, which happened to be uninhabited at the time. They lived there for many generations until there was a famine and they invaded Narnia and conquered it. So not only is Caspian king by his Telmarine lineage—but also because he is actually a descendant of Earth (and thereby a son of Adam) he can truly join the King Club of Narnia.

I have to admit I was feeling a little woozy after wading through Aslan's "explanation." Is this because I'm an adult? Or is it just my personal taste?

While all that is a fanciful yarn and some readers might be pleased with it, I can't help thinking that with more time spent considering the possibilities, a mind as brilliant as Lewis' could have come up with something more interesting, exciting and, above all, plausible.

✎ An Invitation to the Dance ✎

Spiritual Commentary by Kathy Bledsoe

*If my people, who are called by my name, will
humble themselves and pray and seek my face and
turn from their wicked ways, then will I hear from
heaven and will forgive their sin and will heal their
land.*   —2 Chronicles 7:14

The land of Narnia has descended into spiritual darkness.
Only a remnant of believers in Aslan remains and Narnia is no
longer graced with Aslan's physical presence. The High Kings and
Queens have disappeared. Talking animals, good giants, dwarfs,
"living" waters and talking trees still exist—but they are
subsisting on fear or dwelling in hiding. A cruel and heathen race
has conquered the land and established its dynasty upon the
throne. Thousands of years have passed and Cair Paravel is in
ruins. The Golden Age of Narnia is over. Desperate times call for
desperate measures.

Though neither readers nor the Pevensie children
themselves yet realize it, *Prince Caspian* opens with the most
desperate measure mankind has available: an appeal to the
Creator—the simple prayer for help. Scripture is rife with the
examples of prayers lifted by God's people in all circumstances,
but prayers are never so poignant as when backs are against the
wall and situations seem hopeless.

When Doctor Cornelius sends Caspian away from Miraz's
court, he presses a horn into the boy's hands, explaining that its
sound is purported to bring strange and powerful help—even
perhaps the appearance of Aslan himself. This is the magic horn
of Queen Susan, Aslan's particular gift to her, left behind in
Narnia when she vanished at the end of the Golden Age. Caspian
is also warned to use the horn only at his "greatest need." Later,
deep in Aslan's How, a secret, ancient, magical place, Caspian

and his advisors realize that the defeats they have suffered against Miraz's army have brought them to such a point of desperation and need. They can do no more on their own. They will sound the horn. The call for help will go out. However, Caspian's war council determines that the call, or prayer if you will, could be answered in any of three sacred places—Aslan's How, Lantern Waste, or the castle at Cair Paravel—so the council dispatches trusted messengers to the other two places in order to be ready to receive whatever help arrives.

At this point in the story, through several of his characters, Lewis reveals some common attitudes about prayer—for which the blowing of the horn stands as a metaphor. Doctor. Cornelius, for instance, details the mystery of prayer: a source of "strange help—no one can say how strange."[†] When we pray, there is no guarantee of an answer; nor is there a promise of an answer that we expect, or even one that makes sense at the time. Sometimes a fear of the unknown wheels which prayer might set in motion can actually compel us to hesitate—or even to refuse to take action through prayer. Even disappointment in the manner in which previous prayers were answered (or perceived not to be answered at all!) can discourage further prayer completely.

But Cornelius leads Caspian to understand that the "gift" of the horn is not to be wasted because of doubt, fear or indecision. This mirrors Lewis' belief that prayer is, above all, a mystery that cannot be completely explained or controlled. In *Letters to Malcolm: Chiefly on Prayer*, Lewis goes so far as to wonder if "prayer, in its most perfect state, is not a soliloquy, God speaking to God."[‡] He cites the text of Romans 8:26, which tells us that "the Spirit helps us in our weakness. We do not know what we ought to pray for, but the Spirit himself intercedes for us with groans that words cannot express." Lewis believed that the "Holy Spirit guides our decisions from within when we make [prayers]

[†] C. S. Lewis, *Prince Caspian*, p. 58.
[‡] C. S. Lewis, *Letters to Malcolm: Chiefly on Prayer*, p. 68.

with the intention of pleasing God."[†] This seems to be the point Doctor Cornelius is also making to Caspian. Don't worry about the how, why, and wherefore... just use the tool you've been given. Certainly we can understand that Aslan would not be pleased at the state of Narnia under the Telmarines.

Cornelius also reveals the power of prayer, the power to bring great help and "set all to rights." Indeed, the Bible tells us in Ephesians 6 that we are to "pray in the Spirit on all occasions with all kinds of prayers and requests." Aslan has left a powerful tool that can summon either him or his agents when the true Narnians understand that they absolutely have no power to effect the salvation of their land. God wants to hear from us; and, as Blaise Pascal says, God instituted prayer in order "to communicate to His creatures the dignity of causality."[‡] The "creature" is allowed to "assist" the Creator, so to speak, through the exercise of "free will." Lewis explains this well in *God in the Dock*:

> [God] invented both prayer and physical action for
> [the dignity of causality]. He gave us small creatures
> the dignity of being able to contribute to the course
> of events in two different ways. He made the matter
> of the universe such that we can (in those limits) do
> things to it; that is why we can wash our own hands
> and feed or murder our fellow creatures. Similarly,
> He made His own plan or plot of history such that it
> admits a certain amount of free play and can be
> modified in response to our prayers.[§]

Reepicheep the Mouse reveals the truth that prayer can affect God's course of action. Biblically, the most blatant example we have is when Moses pleads with the Lord to spare the nation of Israel. Just as Moses kept arguing with God for the souls of the

---

[†] C. S. Lewis, *Letters to Malcolm: Chiefly on Prayer*, p. 21.

[‡] Blaise Pascal, *Pensees*, No. 513.

[§] C. S. Lewis, *God in the Dock*, p. 106.

children of Abraham, Isaac and Jacob, Reepicheep asks for the return of his tail. At first Aslan tests him by pointing out that he may be taking a little too much pride in his dignity and honor, but Reepicheep regains his tail when his followers demonstrate a willingness to sacrifice their own tails out of love for their leader. Greater love has no one than this, that he lay down his life (or his tail?) for his friends (see John 15:13).

Trumpkin the dwarf, meanwhile, is a portrait of the skeptical agnostic. Today we might hear someone like him say, "I don't believe that prayer will change anything because I don't know if there is anything or anyone out there to effect such change; but if it makes you feel better I won't stop you from talking to the air." He reminds me of the times I have gently told non-believers, "You may not believe in God, but that doesn't keep Him from believing in you." But the force of Caspian's "prayer" impacts even Trumpkin. He hears a sound that he will never forget: "loud as thunder," "cool and sweet as music over water," "strong enough to shake the woods."[†] Eventually, Trumpkin even comes face-to-face with the living answer to this powerful call for help. The encounter does not make him an immediate believer, but it definitely influences a step toward Aslan rather than away from him.

Peter and the other children literally embody the often irresistible force of God's will in answering prayer. But Lucy alone understands that Aslan is at the root of their being literally dragged back into Narnia from a British train station; the other three attribute the call to forces of magic. Modern mankind (self-assured of being enlightened) pooh-poohs the idea of unseen spiritual forces working in response to a bunch of co-dependent "crackpots" talking to some invisible deity. The preferred alternative is to name whatever occurs as luck or coincidence or karma. Yet the true believer in the power of prayer sees them as "God incidents." Somehow, only Lucy has retained a vestige of the faith she found in Aslan after the children's initial trip through

---

[†] C. S. Lewis, *Prince Caspian*, p. 94.

the wardrobe. The others seem to have become dulled to Aslan's purpose and, in fact, his very existence. A year in the "real" world has done much to "erase" the memories of the many years spent in the service of Aslan in Narnia.

The Pevensie children and Reepicheep also represent proof of God's unexpected answers to prayer. Trumpkin assumes that the call will bring great warriors, not children or—heaven forbid—mice! How in Narnia will such a desperate war be won with such puny reinforcements? Three great scriptural truths give the answer:

"For my thoughts are not your thoughts, neither are your ways my ways," declares the Lord.
—Isaiah 55:8

But God chose the foolish things of the world to shame the wise; God chose the weak things of the world to shame the strong. —1 Corinthians 1:27

I can do everything through [Christ] who gives me strength. —Philippians 4:13

The children already know from previous experience that Aslan is not a "tame" lion. They have also learned that he is not predictable or controllable. The air of Narnia "works" on the children enabling them to "mature" again into adults—and strengthening them for the task to which they have been called.

All of Aslan's subjects waver in their faith at some point or in some way, and yet they are used powerfully in both their spiritual and physical weaknesses to bring Aslan's will to fruition. Some of them recognize that power at work in and through them. Some of them don't see it or understand it until they come physically face-to-face with Aslan. Reepicheep, the smallest and seemingly most foolish, is in fact the most righteous, courageous and true. Caspian, in humility and defeat, calls for help. It is a process that Lewis called The Great Dance—and prayer is but the invitation.

The Great Dance is a metaphor for the believer's relationship with God. This relationship is something that God desires but does not force upon those He has created. God gives every person the right to freely choose His company. Yet any relationship that will be strong, true and beneficial to both parties requires good communication. Good communication requires conversation. Prayer, by its simplest definition, is conversation with God. The deeper the conversation, the stronger the relationship becomes.

Lewis experienced the power of prayer and understood its impact on the life of a Christian, so we should not be surprised to find an expression of his faith in this powerful tool over and over in the pages of his writing. But Lewis did not arrive at this understanding easily, and he admits in *Surprised By Joy* that he was "brought into the Faith kicking and struggling and resentful with eyes darting in every direction looking for an escape." He goes on to call faith a paradox because although one is given free will to come to God, the surrender still feels like a "deeply compelled action. I chose, yet it really did not seem possible to do the opposite."[†] Likewise, many characters in the *Chronicles of Narnia* express the inability to resist the "pull" of Aslan. In *Mere Christianity*, Lewis explains it thusly:

> God is not a static thing but a dynamic, pulsating activity—a life or a kind of drama. He is almost a kind of dance. The whole dance or drama or pattern of God's three-personal life is to be played out in each one of us. Or... each one of us has got to enter that pattern. We must take our place in the dance.[‡]

Even though Lewis never meant the Narnia books as theological instruction, *Prince Caspian* develops not only into an outlet for the author's struggle to accept and enter the dance, but it also becomes an example of the journey that every believer

---

[†] C. S. Lewis, *Surprised by Joy*, p. 215.
[‡] C. S. Lewis, *Mere Christianity*, p. 152f.

must make.

Lucy, for instance, exemplifies the faith of a child—accepting, willing to suspend any question of disbelief. She also holds that bright coal of faith that glows deep within and smolders back to life even after a long absence from the "conversation."

Nikabrik portrays the angry Lewis who broke with God and became an atheist in the years following the death of his mother. Caspian says Nikabrik has "gone sour inside from long suffering and hating."[†] Lewis describes the years of his own atheism as hate-filled and dark. Sometimes the tragedies and disappointments of life cause believers to decide that we do not need God and can run our own lives, thank you. Placing blame with the Creator is often the beginning of the break and involves much time spent as a wallflower—feigning indifference or desperately wishing that God would come and sweep us back onto the dance floor.

Trumpkin represents the period when Lewis became exhausted with trying to maintain his hatred of God and tried to just exist as an agnostic. In effect, the emotionally exhausted believer (or skeptic) throws up his hands and says, "I'm done with this. It doesn't matter if God exists or not."

Peter, Edmund and Susan represent Lewis' (and the reborn believer's) journey back to living faith, a faith that had never completely died but whose spiritual muscles needed reformation and strengthening. Each person goes through different experiences and meets God in personally specific ways—ways that are that person's story and nobody else's. Every person's relationship with the Creator is unique, private, and shared with no one else, as Aslan taught in *The Horse and His Boy*.

The badger, Trufflehunter, is the picture of the mature believer, the assured and unshakable spiritually grown Lewis, who lived out his adult life in relationship with and service to his God. Trufflehunter is an example of a believer who trusts that

---

[†] C. S. Lewis, *Prince Caspian*, p. 168.

"help will come," that "it may be even now at the door."[†]

When the prayer is answered... when Aslan returns... when Narnia is saved, Aslan and the children "make holiday," dancing and reveling through the countryside with great joy: for their relationship with each other and with Narnia has been restored. In *Letters to Malcolm*, Lewis describes this scene:

> In this valley of tears certain qualities of Heaven have no chance to get through, can project no image of themselves, except in activities that for us, here and now, are frivolous. How can one find any image of boundless freedom in the serious activities either of our natural or of our present spiritual life? It is only in our "hours off," only in our moments of festivity, that we find an analogy. Dance and game are frivolous, unimportant on Earth, for Earth is not their natural place. Here they are a moment's rest from the life we were created to live. In this world everything is upside down. That which, if it could be prolonged here, would be a truancy is like that which, in a better country, is the goal of all goals. Joy is the serious business of Heaven![‡]

This serious business of Heaven, this joy, comes with an invitation for all to enter the Dance. At the end of *Prince Caspian* all prayers (even the unspoken) are welcomed and answered: Narnia is returned to the "true" Narnians; the tree people and water people are free to come out in the open; the talking animals, giants, fauns and dwarfs do not have to flee over borders or live underground; Caspian, a true Son of Adam, is back on the throne; and the Telmarines who wish to depart are returned to the world they never were meant to leave.

In the plan of the Great Dance plans without number interlock, and each movement becomes in

---

[†] C. S. Lewis, *Prince Caspian*, p. 158.

[‡] C. S. Lewis, *Letters to Malcolm: Chiefly on Prayer*, p. 92f.

its season the breaking into flower of the whole design to which all else has been directed. Thus each is equally at the center and none are there by being equals, but some by giving place and some by receiving it, some things by their smallness and the great by their greatness, and all the patterns linked and looped together by the unions of a kneeling with a sceptred love. Blessed be He!
—from *Perelandra*[†]

For the dance is love itself. The Great Dance does not exist for us but we for it.
—from *The Problem of Pain*[‡]

[†] C. S. Lewis, *Perelandra*, p. 217.
[‡] C. S. Lewis, *The Problem of Pain*, p. 153.

The Voyage of the *Dawn Treader*

One criticism of C. S. Lewis' *Chronicles of Narnia* that would be almost impossible to defend is that he repeats himself. Each of the seven books has its own character, its own unique flavor and style.

It's true enough, in one sense, that *The Voyage of the* Dawn Treader "picks up" the storyline of *Prince Caspian*, giving us a glimpse of Caspian's reign as King of Narnia. And while it's also true that Caspian's character is only here fully realized, *Voyage* is still no retread of the earlier books. In this story, we go to sea and are entertained in the fashion of classic episodic tales like *The Odyssey* and *Gulliver's Travels*. We haven't seen the likes of this in the *Chronicles* before.

Two Roads through Narnia

Paul McCusker, writer and director of the recent *Chronicles of Narnia* production from Focus on the Family Radio Theatre, has pointed out the problems of adapting the books in a different order from that in which they were first published.[†] To a certain extent, he says, *Voyage* works best when taken as the third book in the series. It offers an oddly apocalyptic vision of the literal "end of the world." But McCusker also points out that *Voyage* has the advantage of being the most literarily "mature" of the original three stories—and that Lewis further invested the story with a certain narrative weight since he conceived it as the "final" book in the series. It was not originally meant to be the "middle" of the broader tale.

So in *The Voyage of the* Dawn Treader, we find Lewis at the peak of his story-telling game, and we also find compelling and moving themes. This time around, George brings us our story synopsis and Kathy entertains us with a review of the literary themes of the story in an imaginative fashion consistent with the creativity of Lewis' tale. Finally, Jenn uses Lewis' imagery of the episode at the Dark Island as a jumping-off point for a meditation on how the spirituality of the novel has interlaced with her own life.

Enjoy!

[†] Paul McCusker, unpublished telephone interview with Greg Wright.

❧ Sailing the Pevensies ❧

Synopsis by George Rosok

As a new summer begins, the Pevensie children have been split up. While Peter and Susan are away, Edmund and Lucy go to stay with their cousin, Eustace Scrubb. Eustace doesn't like his cousins very much, and frankly, the feeling is mutual. Eustace is an annoying child who likes to bully people and generally be a royal pain, unlike Lucy and Edmund—who are just royal.

One day Lucy and Edmund begin reminiscing about Narnia while looking at a painting of a sailing ship. True to form, Eustace teases them and moves toward the picture wanting to smash it. Edmund springs after him because he knows magic is at work. Lucy grabs at Edmund and they all fall into the picture and then into the sea.

They are quickly rescued. Onboard the *Dawn Treader*, the Pevensie children find that their rescuer is their friend Caspian, the King of Narnia. Edmund and Lucy are overjoyed, but Eustace is cranky and wants to go home, especially after he encounters Reepicheep, the valiant mouse. Eustace hates mice.

Caspian explains that the purpose of his voyage is to search for the seven lords who had been sent by his late uncle Miraz to explore the unknown Eastern Seas. Reepicheep has an even higher hope—to find Aslan's country at the eastern end of the world. Eustace's goal is to stay in his cabin and be seasick, but (to his great consternation) Lucy cures him of his seasickness with a drop from her diamond flask, which Caspian has most fortuitously brought along.

Their first port is Felimath of the Lone Islands, where the landing party is captured by slave traders. Fortunately, Caspian is quickly sold to an honest-looking man who turns out to be the first of the lost Seven, Lord Bern and the pair rejoin the *Dawn Treader* on the other side of Felimath. The ship's company arrives on the neighboring island of Doorn, where they confront the corrupt governor, who is removed by Caspian and replaced by Bern. At the slave market, they free all the slaves, including Edmund, Lucy, Reepicheep—and Eustace, whom no one would have even for free.

After refitting the ship, they set sail for unknown waters. One evening a storm comes up behind them very fast and lasts for days, badly damaging the ship. Now in a dead sea, they are forced to ration water. Eventually Eustace becomes desperate enough to try to steal some water, but Reepicheep, who is guarding the water supply, catches him. Eustace is forced to apologize, and Caspian warns that anyone else caught trying to steal water will get "two dozen"—and he doesn't mean Krispy Kremes.

Finally, the wind comes up again and after a few days they reach an island of tall mountains. The ship's company goes ashore, and after refreshing themselves they start the work of repairing and replenishing the ship. Unsurprisingly, Eustace decides he deserves some rest and sneaks off into the mountains. Soon clouds close in and he finds himself in an unknown valley. To make matters worse, he discovers that he is sharing the valley with a tired, old-looking dragon, which presently rolls over and dies in a pool of water. When rain begins to fall, Eustace dashes to the dragon's cave. There he finds treasure, including a jeweled band that he pushes onto his arm before lying down on a pile of coins and going to asleep. As he wakes, he is horrified to realize that he has actually become a dragon himself.

Meanwhile, distraught by Eustace's disappearance, the others mount a search party. Their distress increases significantly when they spot a dragon flying over the trees above them. The dragon lands on the beach, and in the morning Caspian and company approach expecting a battle, but find the dragon has no desire to fight. In fact, it is in pain from the armband that is now very tight on its big dragon arm. Caspian sees by its markings that the armband belonged to Lord Octesian, another of the missing Seven. Before long they discover that the dragon can understand what they are saying, and after many questions determine that the dragon is actually Eustace, who is extremely remorseful over how he had behaved before and now becomes very helpful.

Early one morning, Edmund wakes to find Eustace restored to human form. The one-time dragon describes how during the night a great lion appeared and led him to a garden at the top of a mountain. There the lion freed him from his scaly skin, bathed and clothed him, and returned him to the edge of the wood. Edmund explains that Eustace has seen Aslan. From this point forward, Eustace begins to be a better boy. He still has lapses, but his healing has begun.

They soon set sail, and after a narrow escape from an enchanted spring which had turned a third missing lord into solid gold, they come to an inhabited island. After landing, the company finds a path leading to a quiet-looking house. As they follow the path, Lucy falls behind to get a rock out of her shoe and hears a loud thumping approach her. Then she hears voices around her, but she can't see anyone. The Thumpers are invisible. The voices state they are going to attack the company from the *Dawn Treader*. Hastily, Lucy goes to warn the others. They confront the invisible Thumpers at the beach and find out that they had made themselves invisible because the magician that lives in the house put an "uglifying" spell on them. Now, as unhappy with invisibility as they were with being "uglified," they want Lucy to read a spell to make them visible again.

Her companions advise against it, but Lucy agrees. The next morning, Lucy goes upstairs in the house to a room where she finds the Magic Book. After nearly becoming enchanted herself, she finds the spell and makes everyone visible again— including Aslan. Lucy is very happy to see the Lion, who introduces her to the magician before taking her out to meet the now-visible Duffers. At first she thinks there are many odd-looking large mushrooms on the lawn, but when the clock chimes three, they roll over and stand up. These are the Duffers: "monopods," with one thick leg and an enormous foot, who must jump to move thumpingly about. The rather simple Duffers like the name Monopods, but they keep getting it wrong, eventually settling on the misnomer "Dufflepuds."

After the fourth of the missing Seven is picked up at sea off the shore of a mysterious Dark Island, the party comes to another island where they find a table laid with an amazing feast. At one end of the table sit three men, asleep and overgrown with their own hair. Eeww! But these are the remaining missing lords. During the night, a tall, beautiful girl comes out of a doorway in the hillside, and tells them that the lords were put to sleep because they quarreled and became violent. Reepicheep drinks to the lady and dines; the others soon follow suit.

Presently an old man also walks out of the hillside. He comes to his daughter and they begin to sing beautifully. Soon the gray clouds in the east lift and the sun rises. Large white singing birds fly to them and land on everything, even the travelers. The birds consume the remainder of the feast and fly away. Finally the old man turns to the travelers and welcomes them. Caspian asks him how they can remove the enchanted sleep from the lords, and Ramandu informs them that to do so they must sail to the world's end, returning only after leaving at least one of their company behind, never to return into the world—which is Reepicheep's one desire.

After leaving Ramandu's island, they notice that they do not need to sleep or eat as much, and that there is a great deal of light. The sun is much larger here. The sea water is also very clear and potable—"drinkable light." Before long they also discover that although there is no wind, they continue to move eastward at a steady clip. While gazing into the crystalline water, Lucy finds a race of sea-people who dwell on the ocean floor.

Eventually they become aware of a whiteness stretched along the horizon. They send out a small boat and the party returns bearing lily blossoms: indeed, the whiteness is an ocean of lilies as far as the eye can see. They row the *Dawn Treader* for several days through the lilies. The water becomes shallower, and eventually they can go no farther. Caspian calls everyone on deck, declaring their mission to be at an end; he then announces, to great astonishment, that he intends to accompany Reepicheep.

Edmund and Reepicheep insist that he must not, that it would be breaking faith with his loyal subjects if he did. Not used to being contradicted, Caspian becomes rather upset, and withdraws to his cabin after a bit of a tantrum.

Caspian's discontentment grows when Aslan appears to him privately and tells him that he is to return home at once; Reepicheep, Edmund, Lucy and Eustace are to go on by themselves. There is a grievous parting. A boat with the final four travelers is let down and continues east. The *Dawn Treader* turns and begins rowing west. As a third day dawns Reepicheep and the children see the sun rising through a stationary wave. Beyond the wave and the sun is a huge range of mountains that they determine must be Aslan's country.

Reepicheep says this is where he goes on alone. He takes off his sword, which he says he will need no more, and tosses it across the lilied sea, where it sticks upright with its hilt above the surface. He bids the others good-bye, gets into his own small vessel, and paddles into the current where he is taken up and over the wave. Eustace, Edmund and Lucy begin wading south along the wave; the water gradually becomes shallower until there is sand and then a flat lawn. They walk until they meet a lamb, who invites them to a breakfast of fish.

Suddenly the lamb becomes the Lion Aslan. The children are all very happy to see him, but their joy is cut short when he tells Edmund and Lucy that they will not be returning to Narnia, though they will see him again. As for Eustace, Aslan will not reveal whether or not the boy will come back. The Great Lion then opens a door in the sky, and the children find themselves at long last back in the bedroom at Cambridge. And Eustace is a changed boy.

❧ Imagination ÷ Creativity = 1 ❧

Literary Analysis by Kathy Bledsoe

I am just thrilled to present an exclusive interview that I was able to score with the characters of C. S. Lewis' *The Voyage of the* Dawn Treader. Recently, I spent a delightful afternoon discussing this wonderful sea tale with Kings Caspian and Edmund, Queen Lucy, Eustace Scrubb and Reepicheep the brave and chivalrous mouse. Speaking with them personally opened up new vistas of understanding regarding this terrific children's fantasy—and the fertile imagination of Mr. Lewis, which created the plot and this ensemble of characters...

KB: First of all, welcome! I am so excited to spend time with you and am truly blessed to have such an amazing opportunity. I hope that your journey here was easy and eventless. You don't look any worse for the wear...

Lucy Pevensie: Thank you, Kathy. This is quite an occasion. I daresay that Caspian and Reep may be a bit shaken since they have not had a lot of experience traveling between worlds, but speaking for myself, such travel is becoming rather a commonplace occurrence.

Edmund Pevensie: Yes, and tele-transportation is infinitely to be desired over being dumped into a frigid sea. Walking through a wardrobe, while strange, is a much drier proposition!

King Caspian: [Staring around as though completely befuddled] This is amazing. I've known Edmund, Lucy, Susan and Peter... well, and Eustace... to come and go without warning, but I've always written it off as their being a bit daft (though in a good sort of way) and never really worried myself about it. Wait until Drinian and Rhince hear about this!

Eustace Scrubb: Is that a computer?! I never thought I'd ever have the opportunity to see one so small. There aren't any wires. How does it work?

KB: *It's called a "laptop." I'd be glad to show it to you after the interview...*

Reepicheep the Mouse: Far be it from me to sound rude, but I was called from a place that I really had no desire to leave, and would like to return as soon as I possibly can. Could we please proceed with our purpose?

LP: Dear, dear Reep, always calling us back to focus. What would we do without him?

KB: *Yes, point well taken, Reepicheep. Let us proceed with the task at hand. I know that you all have pressing matters to return to in your own realities.*

One of the initial things that I noticed in this story that is quite different from the others (except, to a certain extent, The Horse and His Boy*) is that Lewis spends much more time describing his characters. For instance, in* The Lion, the Witch and the Wardrobe, *we received one-liners here and there about the characters that, yes, did reveal traits, but we mostly learned who the characters were by their actions and often had to discover their true identities by how they interacted with other characters. We learn more about Eustace Scrubb in the first few pages of chapter one of* Voyage *than we did about many of you in the reading of entire books prior to this one.*

ES: [Wryly] And dash it all... he insisted on including my middle name! Eustace is bad enough, but Eustace Clarence is only what my parents called me. I was quite the rotter, wasn't I? But when one thinks about it, Lewis had to really be careful and develop his characters fully or the entire story would have gone nowhere. During the course of this tale, I undergo a complete turnabout of who I am. If the reader did not know me well, the impact of the change would have been completely buried and lost, or at the very least seemed contrived. I think Lewis was so exacting and detailed because the lessons of this book were somehow more important than ever to him and he didn't want obscurity to cloud the message.

RM: Quite, quite, but I believe that there is something more profound going on with Mr. Lewis in this book. I believe that he was maturing as a writer of children's fantasy fiction. After all, Mr. Lewis had the examples of great imaginations like George MacDonald, Lewis Carroll and John Bunyan to guide him. He respected their contributions and considered Mr. MacDonald to be a mentor and guide for his own development as a children's author. Moreover, both Mr. Lewis and Mr. MacDonald passionately believed that a children's book could not be great unless it was equally enjoyed by any person (or mouse) of any age. An adult will see right through a poorly-developed story with one-dimensional characters and never pick it up again. *Prince Caspian* is a close call! (No offense, I hope, Sire.)

EP: Yes, yes... and I recently read an interesting article by Trevor Hart in *Christian History & Biography* which illuminated George MacDonald's belief that since we are made in God's image, imagination must be a part of that image, and that our imaginations are "nothing other than a direct reflection of God's own creativity."[†]

KC: Hear, hear, Edmund! Well read, indeed! [Evokes laughter from the group and Edmund blushes.]

LP: Careful, Caspian... you're sounding like a Dufflepud! [More laughter]

KB: *Okay, okay, we are beginning to drift. Reepicheep, I'd like to go back to something you were saying about the*

[†] Trevor Hart, "The Wise Imagination," *Christian History & Biography*, Issue 86, Spring 2005.

The Voyage of the Dawn Treader

writer's maturity. Your character also becomes more "fleshed out" in this book. How do you account for that?

RM: Again, learned miss [Kathy now blushes], I believe it was due to maturity. *Prince Caspian* (the book) was a great disappointment for me. I was like a caricature—the very type of rodent [said with complete disdain] found in your modern day cartoons rather than the symbol of courage and chivalry that I truly am. Aslan recognized those traits and to some extent so did the children, but it was like Mr. Lewis just didn't take me seriously even though my fellow mice had been given a very important role at Aslan's sacrifice. In *The Voyage of the* Dawn Treader, I am finally a fully-exposed character. And, instead of "popping" in and out of the action, I am made the carrier of the greatest quest and allowed to sacrifice myself for that purpose. I am also the compass that keeps the quest alive and reminds the other characters to stay focused.

KC: [Nudging Edmund] Bet that was hard to do when Eustace had you swinging around by your tail, Reep!

RM: I will not dignify that remark with a response. If I had not tossed my rapier into the sea of lilies, you would taste the flat of it now for sure! Mr. Lewis did have his fun with all of us in this book and, upon his arrival in Aslan's country, I was able to speak to him about that. He is most contrite!

ES: Will everyone just forget that happened? I was different then!

RM: While I forgive you, sir, I will never be able to forget such an indignity...

LP: Gentlemen, gentlemen. You've had your fun, but even you, Reep, are losing focus. I think that maturity of the writer is a valid point, but there is also something more profound happening in this book. Mr. Lewis falls in love with his characters.

EP: Lucy, have you gone bonkers?

KC: Leave it to a girl to go off on a romanticizing expedition!

RM: Lady Fair has a right to her opinion, and though skeptical, I will hear it.

KB: *Yes, I'm intrigued. Please Lucy, elucidate.* [Get it? E-luci-date?]

LP: What I mean by falling in love is that Lewis seems to have real affection for his characters. It is as if he has made friends with every one of us. We are more real and believable characters. Our interaction with each other is true-to-life and typical of people familiar with each other. The reader gets a sense that Lewis really liked this book. He is more playful with his dialogue, pays more attention to detail, clarifies points throughout the story and paints wonderful word pictures that stir the reader's imagination. Long before Lewis wrote the Narnia books, he penned a very good book entitled *The Four Loves...*

KB: *Oh, yes, I've read that and I think I know where you are going with this. Please continue.*

LP: In *The Four Loves,* Lewis speaks of *storge* [two syllables, "hard" g], or affectionate love, as a paradox of need and gift-love.[†]

EP: How's that?

LP: Affection needs to give but it also needs to be needed, and so seeks the gift of being loved. Lewis gives us meaningful life and in the process experiences deep affection for each of us that is demonstrated in all the points I have just made. Just look at the diversity among the characters of this book. How could a human carbuncle like Eustace Scrubb...

ES: I am rather jewel-like, aren't I?

EP: I think she means the other carbuncle, Scrubbsie!

[†] C. S. Lewis, *The Four Loves*, p. 11.

ES: Hey!

LP: Sorry, Eustace, you just make such a good object! How could a Eustace Scrubb become a member of such a band of close friends? How could Reepicheep or even Caspian accept him into their circle? Why would Edmund and I not just isolate him and forget about him and go on with the task at hand? Why does Lewis even have to bring Eustace into the story? Because of what Lewis calls the "glory of Affection," which "can unite those who most emphatically, even comically, are not; people who, if they had not found themselves put down by fate in the same household or community, would have had nothing to do with each other."[†] Lewis is the "fate" who brings about the miracle of affection amongst this ensemble and, I believe, in the process finds himself loving not only the work of writing the story but is surprised by the joy (sorry, couldn't resist) of truly enjoying his characters. So he, too, receives a gift—satisfaction and peace.

EP: I agree, and one really telling proof of this is that Lewis, for the first time in the *Chronicles*, makes great use of the first person. He interjects himself constantly into the book and really becomes an additional character. The reader learns a great deal about Lewis, especially his sense of humor, and is made to feel like a participant in the journey. This book makes a great read-aloud because it just literally shouts to be shared. You find yourself wanting to say, "Just listen to this," or "This is so good; can I read you this part?" It's fun being a part of that.

KB: *I agree with what you are all saying, but let me throw a wrench into the works here.*

KC: I say, what's a wrench?

LP: I believe it's just an Americanism, but I'm not sure. These

---

[†] C. S. Lewis, *The Four Loves*, p. 36.

Yanks do have a strange way of speaking sometimes.

ES: She means "spanner."

EP: They have totally destroyed the language, Lewis would say.

KB: *Sorry... What I meant was, allow me to bring up something that seems to contradict this character development that we've been praising. Lucy, Edmund and Caspian almost seem like they aren't needed at all or are just along for the ride. What do you think Lewis was doing with your characters?*

KC: That's pretty easy as far as I'm concerned. I am a bridge character, as are Lucy and Edmund. We share a common history: our adventures in *Prince Caspian*. Lewis would have had to spend a lot of time explaining how Eustace came to be in Narnia (as he did with Shasta and Aravis in *The Horse and His Boy*) if he didn't provide a bridge.

EP: Quite. If the reader has been paying attention to (and has read) prior books in the series, he understands that no one who has come from "our" world stays in Narnia forever. Susan and Peter have already been sent back to come close to their own world and "know [Aslan] better there."[†] You just know that Edmund and Lucy are not going to be spared the same "growing up." Lu and I become the bridge that brings Eustace from one land to the other. The focus is mainly upon him because Aslan has chosen this story and this time for Eustace to begin knowing him "for a little."[‡] That is why Lewis is so careful to describe who Eustace is; otherwise, his eventual change would be meaningless.

LP: Also, remember that the four of us—Susan, Peter, Edmund and I—were pretty insignificant characters in *The Horse and His Boy*, too, but were necessary to keep the book believable as one of the *Chronicles*. It was a departure by

---

[†] C. S. Lewis, *The Voyage of the* Dawn Treader, p. 216.
[‡] Ibid.

Lewis not to include any mention or action out of "our" world; but it was still a rollicking good tale (I believe a Ms. Wright covered that topic elsewhere) that made the world of Narnia believable with its own history and culture.

KB: *Excellent! I see that more clearly now. Very interesting... Let's change directions and talk about the complexity of this book. I would like to know what each of you perceives as the central theme of this story. Reepicheep, would you like to begin?*

RM: Most graciously, fair lady. [Kathy blushes again but is completely taken in by the mouse's manners.] This story is about my quest to fulfill the prophecy spoken over me by a Dryad when I was in my cradle. I am allowed to go on a crusade to find Aslan's country or the end of the world. I am the bravest because I sail fearlessly and doggedly (mousedly?) into the unknown. I am the picture of God's weakest thing making strong things foolish...

EP: Careful there, Reep, your pride is beginning to bulge again.

KC: I beg to differ, Reep. This is the story of *my* quest. Aslan allowed me to swear an oath on my coronation day. I promised that if I was able to establish peace again in Narnia that I would sail away in pursuit of my father's friends and either find them or avenge them. I provided the transportation for Reepicheep, and the rest of you just crashed my party!

ES: You're all wrong! This story is about how I went from being a perfect blighter to being a decent, kind and loving human being, worthy of Aslan's desire to use me further in Narnia.

LP: And, what about me? I learned some very interesting things about myself during this trip and was the instrument Aslan used to free the Dufflepuds from invisibility. Just as they couldn't see themselves, I couldn't see things about myself that needed to be corrected before I could "know Aslan better" in our world.

[Everyone begins talking at once in defense of his or her individual stand and I am forced to restore order.]

KB: *Everyone, everyone, can we not agree that you are all correct? I believe you have discovered yet another of Lewis' devices in this book—the story within a story within a story. [All nod in agreement.] As Aslan has said in previous books, each person's story is his or her own, and subsequently of most importance to that individual. Lewis has written an amazing book that integrates each of your individual stories, uniting them into a complete and balanced scheme that thoroughly delights and instructs.*

Alas, our time is drawing to a close, but I must ask this final question of Lucy and Edmund. Voyage *is where we say good-by to you both until* The Last Battle. *It will next be Eustace Scrubb's and Jill Pole's turn to visit Narnia. What was it like to hear Aslan say that you wouldn't be coming back to Narnia?*

LP: I, as you read, was completely bereft. I wasn't so upset that I would be leaving a fantasy world, but that I would never see Aslan again.

EP: That was my concern, too. How were we to continue on without Aslan in a world such as this?

LP: Of course, Aslan provided the answer as he usually does, courtesy of Mr. Lewis. We have learned to know him here as One "by another name" Who loved us, guided us and prepared us for the time when we finally came to be reunited. And that's not just something artificially tacked on to the story. It's integral.

EP: Still, Lucy, you could not resist asking if Eustace was coming back!

LP: I know... [looking around they all catch each other's eye and say in unison] "not my story!"

[The entire group dissolves into happy laughter and eventually grows quiet.]

KB: *Thank you all so much for your time, your candor, your obvious love for the work you have been a part of, and for your dedication to C. S. Lewis' vision of Narnia. I loved you all when I discovered these books and read them to my son. I have fallen in love with you again as I have read and reread these stories as an adult. Edmund, Lucy... Voyage is a great book to "go out" on; farewell.*

LP: Thank you for having us back.

EP: The pleasure has been mine.

KB: *Reepicheep, Caspian... with pleasure I send you back to Aslan's country.*

RM: [Bows] I am forever at your service, good lady.

KC: [Not to be usurped by a mouse...] And, I, too, am at your service.

KB: *Eustace... I look forward to seeing more of you soon, and so this is not good-by, but ta-ta for now!*

ES: Righto! Now, could I take a look at that computer before I go?

❧ The Dark Island in My Soul ❧

Spiritual Commentary by Jenn Wright

Light... and Darkness

There is something about the basic contrast of light and darkness that nearly always stops me in my tracks. Perhaps my pupils just have extra difficulty constricting, but it goes much deeper than that.

I spent twelve years (half of a lifetime to that point) in a darkness so bleak and devastating that I could not remember what light looked like. Just recently, due to a severe medication reaction, I spent a few weeks back in that dungeon—in agitation, panic, utter darkness.

Having corrected the medication crisis, I am once again thrust into light—and the purest enjoyment of light one can possibly imagine.

So when I read of the unfortunate man who was picked up off of the Dark Island by the *Dawn Treader*, my soul paid attention. Only a mere few hours removed from my own mental midnight, I could empathize with the madness, the wild wide-eyed trauma-ridden expression on his face as he desperately clung to the light and equally desperately abandoned the darkness. Likewise, my thirst for the light seems to steadily increase the farther I get from the darkness. But why? What it is about the nature of light and darkness that can simultaneously elicit fear and relief? Light and darkness are paradoxically and inextricably related in a way that few extreme opposites can be. One simply cannot exist without the other—darkness is the absence of light, and light cannot exist in darkness; thus if you have the one, the other must be somewhere in proximity for the comparison to occur. A marriage of opposites—and, at length, a long separation.

Sailing On

On the verge of light—almost daybreak—awaiting the sunrise... "It's always darkest before the dawn..." That's where *The Voyage of the* Dawn Treader dares to bring the reader (along with the characters)—to the edge of Dawn.

The name of His Majesty's ship (and thus the book) offers significant insight into what comes throughout the story—the quest for Light, treading ever so closely to the Dawn and yet never quite experiencing the awesome sunrise. On the brink of Dawn—the ultimate Dawn, as it is described—with just a taste of its powerful light.

The stated quest, of course, for King Caspian and his crew, is to find the seven men who reluctantly sailed from Narnia years ago to escape the wrath of the usurper Miraz. And in their travels, the crew of the *Dawn Treader* does find the Seven, or at least evidence of their presence. But they are also driven toward adventure—the truest adventure—of finding the edge of the (flat) world, and in this they are equally successful.

But light—the essence of it, its function and especially the experience of it—is addressed by Lewis in perceptive detail, leaving enough to the reader's imagination to perhaps spark a renewed desire for The Light: that is, the Light of Christ.

The Pagan View

The Venerable Bede, a monk from the 7th century, and credited to be the most learned man of his time, described the pagan view of life as a sort of light between two darknesses:

> You are sitting feasting with your aldermen and thanes in winter time; the fire is burning on the hearth in the middle of the hall and all inside is warm, while outside the wintry storms of rain and snow are raging—and a sparrow flies swiftly through the hall. It enters in at one door and quickly flies out the other. For the few moments it is inside, the storm and wintry tempest cannot touch it, but

113

after the briefest moment of calm, it flits from your
sight, out of the wintry storm and into it again.[†]

Rather a bleak picture, though one I am certain captures
the persuasion of many people. Since we do not know what
happens prior to our coming into existence on this earth, and since
we have not yet experienced what comes after our leaving it, it is
perhaps the easiest way to describe the progression of life—the
Unknown being darkness, the Known being light.

But while it may be the easiest description, and the most
readily accepted, there is a strong possibility that it is flat-out
wrong. After all, since we do not know the precise details of what
goes on before birth or after death, how can we possibly assume
that both are places of darkness? Is it not equally easy to imagine
that the light, warm comfort of the feast is actually a regression of
sorts, and that the sparrow continues its flight out the other side
because there is an innate knowledge (or at least hope) that there
is something even better outside the door?

Otherwise, if the sparrow is exiting into darkness, and the
feast is so pleasant and warm, why should he not alight on a
rafter, soak in the heat and nip a few crumbs from the table,
rather than return to the wintry storm?

The Christian View

In *Voyage*, Lewis explores a different fulfillment of the
coming to the edge of the world, beautifully describing the
Christian's journey out of darkness, sitting at the feast and then
entering the fulfillment of light.

The approach toward the Dark Island reaches an intensity
unmatched to this point in the *Chronicles*. We are drawn to the
darkness, wanting to know what it is, yet we, like the sailors, fear
its oppression. Is it necessary to experience the darkness? Why
does Lewis place the darkness here? From my perspective, from

---

[†] Beda Venerabilis (The Venerable Bede), *The Ecclesiastical History
of the English People*, Book II, Chapter 13.

the time the *Dawn Treader* leaves the Dufflepuds and the Magician, the story could be interpreted as Lewis' description of a journey toward Christ—and starkly in contrast to the flight of Bede's pagan sparrow.

The approach of the Darkness is, indeed, frightening, but until they experience the darkness itself, the sailors have no way of knowing how deep is the darkness, how all-encompassing, how difficult to navigate, how dangerous to the psyche. They have known light and they have known darkness, but the definition of true darkness is about to be revealed to them.

Naturally, Caspian questions the sensibility of this—should we dare to enter the darkness? Should we voluntarily sail into complete and utter unknown? It is the question every person must ask himself: Do I want to know what lies in the darkness—in my own darkness? It is a wise question to ask, and I heartily agree, in matters of salvation, with Reepicheep's astute observation that, in such matters, it is a creature's "good fortune not to be a man."[†]

In choosing to venture forward, they lose themselves in the black. Their worst fears are confirmed by Lord Rhoop's rescue, as he rants and raves maniacally in a futile attempt to convince them to turn around. Soon direction is lost, hope is lost, fear nearly takes over as they realize they cannot navigate their own way out of the gloom. Yet just as panic and despair threaten to sink the sailors' psyches, Lucy utters the simplest plea—the first words spoken to Aslan without his visible presence.

And Aslan the Great answers.

Now, it must be noted that just as the plea is the first of its kind, the answer is of a different form from any seen yet. An albatross—a sailor's good omen of deliverance—circles, Aslan in new form, whispering three words into the hopeless darkness surrounding Lucy and the ship's company: *Courage, dear heart.* In an instant her heart is strengthened, the black fades to deep grey, and finally they enter the light again, all with a new appreciation for the blue sky and warm sun and simply the ability

---

[†] C. S. Lewis, *The Voyage of the* Dawn Treader, p. 157.

to see clearly.

Such is the nature of Light.

The End of the World

Throughout the rest of the story, light is a captive theme. When the sailors drink the water, their desires for food and water diminish, and their ability to tolerate the growing light increases in parallel with the brightness of the light itself. Likewise, the more "living water" we take in (see John chapter 4), the more of God's radiance we can not only bear, but appreciate, enjoy, experience fully.

Finally, at the end of the world, the beginning of that Great Light, we know that there is more to the end of this life than darkness. Naturally, Caspian is devastated to learn that he cannot pass through with the Pevensies, as are we who must only imagine what Aslan's land truly holds. But there is certainly a Hope, a palpable sense of excitement, rather than dread of what comes beyond.

Lewis counterpoints the Venerable Bede's sparrow image beautifully here—bringing light to the end of the world, rather than the sparrow's unfortunate flight back into the cold and desolation. In *Surprised by Joy*, Lewis writes:

> The question was no longer to find the one simply true religion among a thousand religions simply false. It was rather, "Where has religion reached its true maturity? Where, if anywhere, have the hints of all Paganism been fulfilled?" ... Paganism had been only the childhood of religion, or only a prophetic dream.[†]

I believe that the vision of light at the end, rather than a flitting comfort bounded by darkness on both ends, is most certainly a more Christ-centered view. We who love this life will lose it (see John 12:25), while those who pursue that greater

---

[†] C. S. Lewis, *Surprised by Joy*, p. 235.

light—at the cost of leaving this world as the Pevensies (and Reepicheep) did—shall find something greater than they have already experienced, not a regression from their earthly experiences.

The journey of the *Dawn Treader* is a picture of the pre-Christian's walk through the recognition of his own sin; the recognition of his need for light; the frantic returning to the light (with a much greater appreciation for it); a thirst which brings about increasingly brighter light (and subsequently increasing awareness of the darkness lurking in our humanity); and ultimately reaching Aslan's land in the brightest light possible, where all is exposed, and none is afraid.

The god of this age has blinded the minds of unbelievers, so that they cannot see the light of the gospel of the glory of Christ, who is the image of God. For we do not preach ourselves, but Jesus Christ as Lord, and ourselves as your servants for Jesus' sake. For God, who said, "Let light shine out of darkness," made his light shine in our hearts to give us the light of the knowledge of the glory of God in the face of Christ. —II Corinthians 4:4-6

The Silver Chair

Though *The Magician's Nephew*, the sixth-written episode in *The Chronicles of Narnia*, is really the book that Lewis designed to "tie up" Narnia's loose ends, *The Silver Chair* has a bit of that feel to it, too. Coming sixth in the chronological sequence as it does, the book, in fact, sets the stage for *The Last Battle*. Principally, it makes the point that the future of Narnia cannot be secured by just making little tweaks here and there, by defeating mere dupes such as Miraz and Rabadash. No, these villains are just pawns in the game of Deep Magic that's being played out between Aslan and his enemies. *The Sliver Chair*, in fact, clarifies that Jadis the White Witch, the first of Narnia's great oppressors, will be neither the last nor the greatest. The

Queen of the Underworld who ensnares Rilian in this tale is just as potent and malevolent.

But *The Silver Chair* doesn't just bring the major themes of the *Chronicles* to a head. This book also connects and continues the story threads of *Prince Caspian* and *The Voyage of the* Dawn Treader, tying the imminent End Times of Narnia back to the beginning of the tale, through the Pevensies to Digory Kirke. *The Silver Chair* is a satisfying conclusion to the overall rising action of the series, working magnificently in its own right as well as preparing us for the *Chronicles'* coming climax.

Lewis here continues the roll he was on in *The Voyage of the* Dawn Treader, offering much food for thought. Kathy leverages her creativity upon our story synopsis, while Jenn and I offer up a collaborative look at how Lewis' craft pays off in the reader's identification with the story's heroes. Finally, George gives us a challenging analysis of the central spiritual symbol of the story: the Silver Chair itself.

Mind the details. . .

✎ Holiday in Harfang ✎

Synopsis by Kathy Bledsoe

Editor: The Silver Chair represents a shift in character focus for the Narnian chronicles. The Pevensie children have all aged beyond recurring magical trips to Narnia, and after his life-changing experiences in The Voyage of the Dawn Treader, *cousin Eustace Scrubb now becomes the main protagonist. Joining him is a school acquaintance, Jill Pole. This synopsis of the story is a compilation of two recently discovered travel diaries—Jill's, and that of a Marsh-wiggle named Puddleglum who was their guide on an amazing journey to find a lost Narnian prince. None other than Aslan himself mandated the quest; and from this point I will allow these two to tell the story.*

Jill Begins...

Yesterday I somehow caught the fancy of the school bullies and was crying behind the gym, where Scrubb found me. He told me an amazing story of a magical place called Narnia, and we both decided to call on the name of someone called Aslan, in order to evade the bullies. We ran to the stone wall at the edge of the school property, and found ourselves looking not onto the dingy moor, but into a dazzlingly bright and sunny different world. Eustace grabbed my arm and pulled me through the door. England vanished and we entered another world.

Before long, we came to the edge of a cliff. Wanting to look brave and make Eustace feel inferior, I looked over the edge to see the tops of clouds and tiny details of a land far below us. Eustace tried to pull me back from the edge but lost his balance and fell. To my utter amazement, a huge lion rushed to the cliff edge and began to blow really hard. It seemed to be controlling Eustace's fall with its breath! As Eustace became a tinier and tinier speck below me, the lion finished blowing and disappeared into a nearby forest. Desperately thirsty, I entered the wood to perhaps find a stream. Well, I found my stream, but right across from me lay that huge lion. He asked me about Eustace and I found that I had to confess that Eustace had fallen off the cliff because of my need to show off. Aslan (for that was his name) also told me that we were both there because he called us—wait, because we called for him. Well, the two are actually the same, I guess.

Aslan gave me four signs needed to complete a quest to find Rilian, the lost Prince of Narnia. He made me repeat them and repeat them until I became very testy, but he admonished that I must be careful to repeat the signs regularly so that I wouldn't forget them. Aslan then also "blew" me into Narnia where I landed near a coastal castle, within a few feet of Eustace. There we saw a frail old king surrounded by courtiers and strange beasts and creatures who had apparently gathered to bid him farewell. The king boarded a ship and set sail. At that point, I tried to tell Eustace the first sign—he was supposed to greet an old and dear friend at once—but we were interrupted by the arrival of a huge owl who took us immediately to the Regent, Trumpkin the dwarf. After I told of Aslan's mission to find the prince, Eustace was sick at realizing that the old friend he was supposed to greet was the king who had just left: that same Prince Caspian in Eustace's Narnia adventure last term. Caspian was now an old man and the father of the lost prince.

After cleaning up, Eustace and I played a great blame-game over the muffed first sign. But late last night, Glimfeather (the owl) flew me to a secret parliament of owls to which he had already delivered Eustace. There we learned how Prince Rilian came to disappear. Ten years earlier, Rilian and his mother the Queen went maying in the north parts of Narnia. While the Queen took a nap, Rilian moved off a ways so as not to disturb her slumber. The Queen's screams drew him to find a great, green snake slithering away. His mother had been bitten on the hand and, despite all of his efforts to save her, she died. Rilian tried to pursue the snake but it escaped through a crack in the ground. Devastated, Rilian began to travel often, tirelessly driven to find and destroy the snake. Eventually he gave up on the search, but became obsessed with a beautiful woman dressed in green. Not long after, Rilian disappeared. The owls were pretty sure that the Green Lady was related to a White Witch who long ago held power in Narnia

This morning, owls carried Eustace and me to the home of the Marsh-wiggles north of Narnia. They can guide us north into Ettinsmoor so that we can satisfy the second sign, which is to "journey to the ruined city of the ancient giants."

Puddleglum Continues

Day One

This morning Jill and Eustace revealed their plan to rescue Prince Rilian, asking for my help. I fully expect to fail at this enterprise but have agreed to be their guide. This will be a long trip. These non-Wiggles argue incessantly!

Day Two

We began the long climb up the rocky moor by the giants' gorge. Silly Jill thought the giants leaning on the edge of the gorge were piles of rocks and I had some real work for a while trying to keep Eustace and her from panicking and getting us all killed. Boulders pelted down around us everywhere but we made it through in relative safety—just to camp on the exposed moor.

Day Nine

Nothing much to write. Living off the land, we have traveled across Ettinsmoor. We were seen by only one giant who just laughed at us and continued on. I'd have laughed, too.

Day Ten

We left the moor today and crossed an enormous giants' bridge that was connected to an ancient roadway. As we came off the bridge, we encountered a mounted, visored Knight in full armor accompanied by a green-clad woman astride a white horse.

I suppose she was gorgeous. She did all the talking, naturally. I had to work hard to keep Jill from giving her too much information. We did find out that the road leads from the bridge to the Castle of Harfang, home of the Gentle Giants. After the lady and her knight were gone, the three of us had a great row. Jill and Eustace made me promise to go to Harfang and I made them promise not to tell the giants about Narnia or Prince Rilian. Jill has quit repeating the signs I have heard her chanting in days past. I'm sure that's a very bad thing!

Undated Entries

Just surviving has kept me from writing on a regular basis. But at last we have come to a plain and can see lighted windows in the distance. One more night of cold camp?

This morning we found ourselves in a driving snowstorm. We climbed a succession of high ledges and encountered a series of baffling dead-end trenches that delayed us for a time. Eustace asked Jill about the signs, but she just said, "Bother the signs." When we spotted the lights again I could not keep them from charging off. We were welcomed into a castle by a very amused giant who had the cheek to call me "Froggy." We were then taken before the King and the Queen. (The Queen was also extremely rude to me.) After Jill burst into tears of utter exhaustion, the three of us were rushed off to bathe, rest and eat.

Today we began the day in Harfang. We looked out a window and realized that the terrain we crossed yesterday in the snow was actually the ruin of a giant city. Those dead-end trenches were actually the carving of the words UNDER ME. We all suddenly realized that Jill's second and third signs had been completely fouled up, too. We then worked out a plan to escape. We could not open the doors because we are so small. Desperate, we discovered that the cook usually leaves the scullery door open a crack for the cat. While we waited for her to drift off into her afternoon nap, Jill found a cookbook with recipes for Man and Marsh-wiggle—and we realized that WE were on the menu for

124

the Autumn banquet! The cook began to snore and we ran out of the castle. A hunting party spotted us and we really had to run for our lives. Fortunately, I spotted a crack in the earth, and we dove in. After filling the opening with rocks, we discovered that we could move deeper into the crevice and stand up. It was so dark that we couldn't see a thing, and suddenly we were all sliding down a long, bone-jarring slope. It was very quiet and very warm and out of the darkness came a peculiar voice.

The "Warden of the Marches of Underland" said we were in the Deep Realm. We were then forced by a company of "Earthmen" to march by a strange, cold light they carried. We continued on through cave after cave until we came to one with water and a ship that we were forced to board. Over and over this Warden had told us that "few return to the sunlit lands" and Jill finally broke under the strain of fear. I reassured her by pointing out that we were under the Ruined City and back on track with Aslan's instructions. This calmed her somewhat.

Finally tonight—this morning?—we came to a bustling port and now have been taken to a great castle to meet the Queen of Underland. Guess who? Yes, the Green Lady. While we await her, we have been talking to the Black Knight, who seems quite delusional. Over dinner the Knight admitted that he was bound by a spell from which only the Lady could free him. Every night (how they tell time I can't imagine—I've completely lost track) the Knight is bound to a silver chair because of some insane fit that makes him a danger to all who are near. The Queen usually attends him until he returns to "normal." The knight has asked us to rejoin him later tonight in the Queen's absence. We shall see.

What a bizarre scene we have witnessed the last few hours! During his fit of "insanity," the Knight commanded us to free him, contradictorily claiming that he was actually sane *only* at this time every night. We resisted until he invoked the name of Aslan—and we realized that this was Jill's last sign. After we freed him, he arose and dashed the chair to pieces with his sword, declaring that he was Rilian, Prince of Narnia, son of the great King Caspian. We had just enough time to explain to him that he had been lost for ten years before we ran smack into the returning Queen. She was very clever and tried to brainwash us with a sweet smelling powder thrown on the fire and a steady, monotonous tune she played on a mandolin. Finally, Jill mentioned Aslan and I stomped my foot in the fire. The pain brought me back to my senses. Well, then things got really interesting! The Queen turned into an enormous green serpent that coiled itself around Prince Rilian's legs. He began to rain blows upon its neck with his sword, and I jumped in with my own (yes, I had remembered to pack a blade); between the two of us we hacked off the beast's head! Rilian's mother's death was finally avenged, and his ten-year enslavement was ended. But boy, am I one tired—and sore—Marsh-wiggle.

Jill Resumes

We managed to find our way back because Rilian told us about a passage to the Overworld only a few miles away. As we planned our retreat, we heard the Earthmen running and shouting as fires reflected on the ceiling of the cavern and the waters of the sea rose into the city. We rescued horses from the stable and rode upward toward the red glow. Puddleglum was able to catch a miserable little gnome who was terrified of us until he learned that the Queen was dead. It turns out that she had enslaved thousands of gnomes from the land of Bism deep in the earth, to work for her in the "Shallow Lands." With the death of the Witch, the gnomes had prepared for war—thinking that the Witch was coming to lead them out to fight in the bright Overworld, and they were going to fight her rather than go out.

We came to the edge of a deep, bright chasm from which emanated a strong but tantalizing smell. Gnomes were everywhere clambering down into this newly-opened entrance to Bism. A voice came from the depths telling all to be quick, saying that the rift was closing. Glog and many other gnomes dove in just before the crack closed and we were left alone in the dim light. We reassumed our ascent. Eventually, we had to dismount as the ceiling lowered. Eustace spotted a tiny patch of light overhead and by standing on Puddleglum's shoulders I was able to find out that it was a hole! And so here we are tonight.

I had managed to get my head out when something hit me in the face. Once my eyes adjusted to the light, I realized that I had come out into the heart of Narnia and had been hit by a snowball. I yelled for help, and the Narnians returned to dig out the rest of the group. There was much joy at our return with Prince Rilian. We ate a good meal and got some rest. Whew!

Last Day in Narnia

When I awoke, Rilian had already gone to Cair Paravel to see his father, whom Aslan had turned back shortly after we had seen him set sail. We said good-by to Puddleglum here, before leaving for the castle ourselves. We arrived at Cair Paravel just as the King Caspian's ship cruised up the river and docked. Then four knights carried the bed-ridden King ashore. Prince Rilian knelt and embraced his father; the King raised his hand in blessing, and his head fell back on the pillows. The King was dead.

Suddenly, Aslan was there, telling us that our job was done and that he had come to take us home. Instantly, we were back on the mountain top where our adventure had begun. Looking into Aslan's stream, we saw the dead King Caspian lying on the bottom and we all wept, even Aslan. But to everyone's surprise (and joy!) Aslan revived Caspian with a drop of his blood; and the King emerged from the water, a young man, fully alive! Aslan sent us back to Experiment House, and granted Caspian five minutes with us in our world. We charged the bullies who had been chasing us when we fled into Narnia. Our headmistress came to see what the ruckus was, going into hysterics over the lion and flying crops and swatting swords, so we took the opportunity to slip back into school while Aslan and Caspian returned to their own world.

Undated Entry

Things have been better here since the headmistress has been removed. The school has become quite good and Eustace and I are, however unlikely, best friends.

❧ Missing the Signs ❧

Literary Analysis by Greg and Jenn Wright

There's much to be said for the value of a close look at a situation—for one thing, it allows you to see just where to place your next step. The close-up is the place where one decides to turn around, choose another route, maybe go back to the beginning and start again. The close-up is an in-the-moment view, where time is of the essence and the split-second decision must be made. Reflection can wait.

But the close-up view is also where doubt may often prevail. Regrets take seed. If only... if only... If only I had the panoramic view—the elusive "Big Picture"—when I made that decision... If only I could have seen then what I saw later. If only I could have known then what I know now.

This Close-Up vs. the Big Picture scenario occurs several times in *The Chronicles of Narnia*, but probably nowhere as prominently as in *The Silver Chair*. Interestingly, this contrast is played out not only with the story's characters, but with the readers as well. When Jill, Eustace and Puddleglum look down on the ruins of the giants' city and see the words UNDER ME, it dawns on them, as well as us, that they had no clue what they were stumbling through in the snowstorm the day before.

But first things first. We're getting ahead of ourselves— one of the tell-tale signs of over-emphasizing the close-up view. To get the scene at Harfang in perspective, we need to remember that the story's characters, to this point, have made a regular habit of missing the Big Picture, particularly regarding Jill and the four "signs" she is given by Aslan.

The first sign—that of Eustace meeting an old friend the moment he steps into Narnia, and Aslan's command that Eustace must greet that friend immediately—is lost precisely because the children get lost in details. Of course, Jill complicates the first sign by showing off at the cliff's edge, causing Aslan to take extra time to convey the signs to Jill instead of to Eustace; and then the boy is subsequently too impatient with Jill to ask the right questions until it is too late. But the major contributing factor in the delay is that both Eustace and Jill become intent on the proceedings of the King's send-off.

Jill's first thoughts upon arriving in Narnia, in fact, have nothing to do with the signs.[†] Instead, "the first thing she thought was how very grubby and untidy and generally unimpressive" Eustace looked. Her second thought? "How wet I am!" For his part, Eustace is so fascinated with "the splendour of their surroundings"—the turreted castle, the white marble quay, the tall, bannered ship and the King's court—that he shuts Jill up with a few cross words when she finally remembers why she's there. "Keep quiet, can't you?" he demands. "I want to listen." Even after Jill gets a word in edgewise about Aslan and his instructions, Eustace curtly tells Jill to "dry up." The children find soon enough, to their complete dismay, that their attention has been sorely misdirected on the setting and ceremonies, while it instead should have been set on the Big Picture: their quest. (Eustace, of course, knew nothing of the quest when Jill arrived; but his past experiences in the world of Narnia, and the unique means by which he was conveyed over the sea, should have led him to believe that something curious was in the cards.)

Gradually, as the days pass since Jill received her instructions about the signs, Jill and Eustace, now traveling with the Marsh-wiggle Puddleglum, once again find themselves steadily becoming more and more focused on the moment at hand. For a time, though, they manage to be devoted to the Big Picture—so much so, in fact, that Jill is oblivious to things close by. She almost entirely misses the fact, for instance, that the "funny rocks" along the edge of gorge leading up to Ettinsmoor are actually the heads of giants. And she habitually recites Aslan's signs twice a day. But as the journey wears on, Puddleglum

---

[†] See C. S. Lewis, *The Silver Chair*, p. 26ff.

becomes more concerned with Aslan's instructions than are the children.

Wearied by travel and chilled through, Eustace and Jill are easily taken in by the invitation by "She of the Green Kirtle" to join the Autumn Feast in Harfang—a lovely place, so she says, with splendid meals, hot baths, warm beds and all the comforts they have thus far been missing.[†] Only Puddleglum, whom Jill accuses of having "the most horrible ideas," thinks to weigh the Lady's words against Aslan's. Yes, only the wet-blanket Marsh-wiggle stops to question the integrity of the Lady, the oddity of the Silent Knight and the too-good-to-be-true welcome into a giants' house. But the children? Jill, by contrast, is simply taken with the Lady's "scrumptious dress. And the horse!" Eustace, impatient with Puddleglum's caution, suggests that they should all just "think about those Gentle Giants and get on to Harfang as quickly as we can." All is forgotten for the promise of a few days' rest for the weary. The close-up view wins out over the Big Picture.

Once again, in fact, myopia becomes the rule. The children can "think about nothing but beds and baths and hot meals," and as the days wear on, Jill forgoes her daily recitations. "She [says] to herself, at first, that she [is] too tired, but she soon [forgets] all about it." In their haste to reach the House of Harfang "not too late," they plow through a snowstorm and have a "beast of day" clambering through "squarish rocks" and a series of ledges. It would be hard enough, in the first place, I suppose, to recognize the ruins of a giant's city; but in a blizzard? Not a chance. Close-up visions of fires, baths and hot food—and the snowflakes in their eyes, and the willfulness in their hearts—blind the children to the Really Big Picture of Aslan's second sign: the ruined city through which they slog.

Soon they fall into strange trenches with odd sharp turns and short dead ends. At first taken in by the respite from the chill winds, the three try to find a through-way—any through-way—to keep them out of sight and out of the dreadful weather. But no

[†] See C. S. Lewis, *The Silver Chair*, p. 75ff.

such luck. Back on the surface again, Puddleglum's suspicions lead him to ask Jill once more about Aslan's signs. "Bother the signs!" she barks. And she incorrectly states that the second sign is "something about someone mentioning Aslan's name." Her retort is rather cross because she knows that she has been less than attentive lately to those important portents. And once the party manages to catch a welcome glimpse of Harfang, the twists and turns of the trenches are quickly forgotten.

Until the next day, when that fateful, Big-Picture panorama of the ruined city below them becomes evident.

Forgetfulness seems to be a major obstacle to the effort of keeping the grand scheme of things in the forefront of one's mind—forgetting the goal, forgetting the steps toward reaching that goal, forgetting everything but the present moment and what might make it more bearable.

Thus, the three travelers unwittingly enter the House of Harfang as the main course for the Autumn Feast. Only after being annoyingly treated like children all night and having a good night's sleep behind them, do they reconvene in the morning in Jill's room to see so plainly from far away what they could not see while they were in the middle of it: that those becalmed trenches spell out, very clearly, UNDER ME. Instantly, regret and shame flush through Jill, as she remembers both the second and third signs—and her disregard for their recitation and focus. The others are also convicted of their own deficiencies: not paying better attention, not recognizing (or speaking up about) the resemblance of the wreckage to a city—about being all too crazy about reaching the House of Harfang, which perhaps never should have sidetracked them in the first place. Generously, Puddleglum avoids saying "I told you so."

But again, myopia is where "little" decisions are made that so often greatly affect the Big Picture. From this point in the story, because of the small but right decisions the party makes, a renewed focus on the signs leads them on a successful quest to find the Prince. When they finally encounter the fourth sign—Rilian's invocation of Aslan's name—they have little problem being convinced that Aslan's instructions must be followed, even though it means breaking the promise they'd made to the enchanted Prince. They free Rilian, and redeem their own failures.

Interestingly, when the Lady enters to find the Silver Chair reduced to shards, she instinctively knows that the best way to confound her enemies' minds is through the senses, those wonderful collectors of details that so often distract us from the Big Picture. Incense and music, magic and a persuasive voice, provide the Lady a near victory in defeating Aslan's schemes. But the Big Picture prevails. Jill does not entirely forget Aslan, and Puddleglum is stirred to stamp out the fire upon which the incense burns. He rightly declares that even if the Witch is right, even if "we have only dreamed, or made up, all those things—trees and grass and moon and sun and stars and Aslan himself," then the made up world—one much bigger than the limitations of the Witch's visible and concrete city—"licks your real world hollow."[†]

Case closed, more or less.

But that brings us back to ourselves, the readers. How smug we are, sitting back and critiquing the children's failures. We, of course, have the luxury of perspective. We can see quite clearly that Jill and Eustace are running the risk of missing the first sign at Cair Paravel. Our only concern: If they actually miss the first sign, how can the quest possibly succeed?

And when the three travelers encounter the Knight and the Lady at the bridge, it's easy for us to think: Gee, why don't Jill and Eustace stop to ponder where these two came from, and where they might be going? Have they forgotten the parliament of owls, and the tale of Rilian's obsession with the "tall and great" beautiful lady, "wrapped in a thin garment as green as poison"?[‡] Could this Knight's lady, "She of the Green Kirtle," be the one and the same? Might it, in fact, be the very same dress?

But these are easy questions for us, the readers. C. S.

[†] C. S. Lewis, *The Silver Chair*, p. 159.
[‡] Ibid., p. 75.

Lewis, like she of the Green Kirtle herself, has worked some very crafty magic on us.

First, we must remember that not all of the volumes in *The Chronicles of Narnia* are written in the same style. *The Silver Chair*, in fact, features some of the most descriptive prose in the series. Why? It might be easy to write it off as a necessary device to enable us to understand why Jill and Eustace are themselves distracted by details. How can we understand their fascination with the ceremony of King Caspian's departure, for instance, unless Lewis describes it for us?

But Lewis is not just showing more consideration for his readers than Steven Spielberg usually does for those watching his films. Lewis is instead providing us with the tools of our own undoing: distracting us with words so that we get caught up in the details of the children's failures and lose sight of the Big Picture lessons that Lewis might have in store. And the magic that Lewis weaves to this end is very effective. We are captured by his web of words. The story works, yes; and we get his point, too. The Close-up View becomes the means to the Big Picture.

Second, as the quest wears on, we, like Jill and Eustace, also become less able to focus on the signs and sort them out in advance. Why? Because Jill's not the only one who stops reciting the signs. Lewis does, too. And unless we bookmark the early passages, our memories become as poor as Jill's. In fact, as Lewis gives us less and less description of the party's surroundings, as the details become more and more focused on what's right in front of the searchers' faces, we—again like them—are just as likely to miss the fact that Harfang lies only a wee bit beyond the ruins that the searchers seek.

Lewis is no fool. Neither are Jill, Eustace and Puddleglum fools. And if we come away from *The Silver Chair* feeling somehow superior to these characters, then we have failed to correctly read the signs that Lewis lays out in this tale—and the Close-up View has won out over the Big Picture.

❧ This Pleasant Darkness ❧

Spiritual Commentary by George Rosok

In chapter eleven of C. S. Lewis' *The Silver Chair,* we find Prince Rilian, sole heir and lost son of King Caspian the Tenth of Narnia, bound tightly to the titular Silver Chair in a dark city deep in the earth. He is urgently pleading with the other protagonists of the story: Eustace Scrubb, whom we met in *The Voyage of the* Dawn Treader; Jill Pole, a schoolmate of Eustace's; and Puddleglum, a Marsh-wiggle from Narnia. Rilian wants them to cut the ropes that bind him and release him from the chair. But they do not know that he is Prince Rilian, the very person Aslan has charged them to seek and bring back to Narnia. Nor do they know that he has been under the spell of a witch, the very witch who killed his mother, the wife of Caspian the Tenth. They only know him, so far, as a silly and cruel knight who is in the thrall of his "queen."

We are all enslaved in darkness in silver chairs. Unlike Prince Rilian, we have each built our own chair, and each chair is as unique as a snowflake. Our guilt, our behaviors, our pasts, our hates, our fears, our possessions—and many other things in varying combinations in varying degrees—bind us to those chairs. Like Rilian, we are sometimes lucid and aware of our predicament but unable to free ourselves because we don't know how. But also like Rilian we are often unaware of our own chair or the spell we are under. We are consumed by our own narrow worldview and are unable to do anything about it because we don't know we are bound. In fact, even when we *are* aware we are often unwilling to change. Further, we do not know that the bonds are largely illusory—that we have, by our choices and beliefs, bound ourselves. Yet ultimately, by choice and belief we can be also be released.

Like the Prince, we look to others to free us; and others can show us the way, even remove the bonds. But how do we get out of the chair—by our own power or by grace or both? And how do we find ourselves in the Silver Chair?

Lewis shows us. Through the journey of Eustace, Jill and Puddleglum we see how they very nearly succumb to the same situation in which Rilian finds himself. Lewis also shows how by their strength and courage, and by the grace of Aslan, they are able to avoid that fate and return to Narnia with Rilian.

In chapter two, Jill is on the Mountain of Aslan. Eustace has fallen off a cliff there, and, although Jill doesn't know it, is safely drifting through the clouds on his way to Narnia. Jill is face-to-face with Aslan and is understandably very frightened. Aslan tells her that Prince Rilian, who has been missing for ten years and has been given up for dead by Caspian and most of Narnia, is alive. Aslan charges her and Eustace to seek Prince Rilian until they have either found him and returned him to his father's house or died in the attempt. To help accomplish this she is given four signs:

> First; as soon as the Boy Eustace sets foot in Narnia, he will meet an old and dear friend. He must greet that friend at once; if he does, you will both have good help. Second; you must journey out of Narnia to the north till you come to the ruined city of the ancient giants. Third; you shall find a writing on a stone in that ruined city, and you must do what the writing tells you. Fourth; you will know the lost prince (if you find him) by this, that he will be the first person you have met in your travels who will ask you to do something in my name, in the name of Aslan.[†]

Before Aslan sends Jill to Narnia to join Eustace, he admonishes her to be sure to remember the signs. Aslan tells her to say them to herself when she gets up in the morning and when she lies down at night. This is reminiscent of Moses' words to the

---

[†] C. S. Lewis, *The Silver Chair*, p. 19f.

tribe of Israel after he has delivered God's laws and commandments: "These commandments that I give you today are to be upon your hearts. Impress them on your children. Talk about them when you sit at home and when you walk along the road, when you lie down and when you get up."[†] Likewise, the four signs are commandments Aslan gives Jill so that she and Eustace will succeed in their quest—much like God's commandments (when followed) would guide the Israelites on their quest to reach Canaan and secure a new life after they arrive.

Aslan also warns Jill that whatever strange things happen, she must let nothing turn her mind from the signs. In Aslan's land her mind is clear, but as she goes into Narnia and farther, "the air will thicken." Finally he gives her a clear and simple instruction: "Remember the signs and believe in the signs. Nothing else matters."[‡]

At first she repeats the signs diligently as she drifts through the clouds to Narnia, but almost immediately after arriving, she and Eustace miss the first sign. Eustace fails to recognize and greet the now-aged Caspian as an old and dear friend. Jill fails to communicate effectively and quickly to Eustace the importance of this sign. Before they can rectify the situation, King Caspian has boarded a ship and has set sail for the Seven Isles, having heard that Aslan may have been sighted there. Israel, we may remember, also immediately failed to follow God's instructions at Mount Sinai, crafting and worshipping a golden calf (see Exodus 32). Jill's and Eustace's failure is not so nearly willful, but the similarity is nonetheless notable.

After meeting Puddleglum and journeying across Ettinsmoor to search for the ruined city of the ancient giants, they miss the second and third signs as well. When they cross the giants' bridge, though they do not realize it, they meet Rilian—who is covered in armor and does not speak. He is with the witch queen, who has put him under her spell. She says she knows

[†] Deuteronomy 6:6-7.
[‡] C. S. Lewis, *The Silver Chair*, p. 21.

nothing about the ruined city and advises the travelers to go to Harfang, a castle in the north where, she says, dwell mild and courteous giants who will give the travelers steaming baths, soft beds and plenty to eat. In fact, she knows these giants will eat Jill, Eustace and Puddleglum if they get the chance—and they very nearly do.

Only the dour Puddleglum is suspicious of this woman. Her advice clouds the minds of the children so that during the hard journey they can think of nothing but the comforts of Harfang. Consequently, as they are struggling across the very ruins they have been instructed to find in Aslan's second sign, they do not recognize them. And even though they are literally inside the letters of the writing of the third sign, they do not realize it.

Jill's failure to remember the signs at this point reminds me of the Parable of the Sower. She is like the rocky soil on which some seeds fell. The seeds "sprang up quickly, because the soil was shallow. But when the sun came up, the plants were scorched, and they withered because they had no root." Jesus elaborates: "The one who received the seed that fell on rocky places is the man who hears the word and at once receives it with joy. But since he has no root, he lasts only a short time. When trouble or persecution comes because of the word, he quickly falls away."[†] At first Jill accepts the signs Aslan has given her and is diligent about remembering and reciting them. But with the passing of time and the increasing difficulty of their journey she falls away from that discipline. Not only does she no longer recite them, she forgets them entirely. Only once they are in Harfang and essentially captives does the party look out a window and see the message "UNDER ME"—and realize that they have missed two more signs.

Nonetheless, they are able to devise an escape from Harfang and follow the instructions of the third sign by going under the ruined city. They are captured deep below the surface

---

[†] See Matthew 13, through verse 21.

by the Earthmen who dwell there, and are eventually joined with Rilian in his chambers in the underground city.

There they are at least able to finally fulfill the fourth sign. While Rilian is bound to the Silver Chair and entreating Eustace, Jill and Puddleglum to release him, he finally invokes Aslan's name. This presents them with a difficult choice, as they promised Rilian before he was bound that under no circumstances would they release him. But once he calls for them to do it in Aslan's name, they choose to do it—even though they believe it may mean their deaths at the hand of this demented knight. They do this not knowing the outcome, but after muffing all the other signs they know they must get this one right even if they are killed. As Puddleglum says, "You see, Aslan didn't tell Pole what would happen. He only told her what to do."[†]

This, of course, turns out to be the right course of action, and Rilian immediately destroys the Silver Chair and announces his true identity. But as in life, this is far from the end of their difficulties. They are barely able to enjoy the success of finding Rilian and freeing him from his spell before the witch enters the chamber. She does not, as one might expect, fly into a Jadis-like rage and start destroying more furniture when she sees Rilian is no longer under her spell. Instead, she plays a mandolin-like instrument and puts a green powder on the fire that produces a pleasant scent, speaking softly all the while.

Rilian tells her that he and the others will leave at once for Narnia. She argues that there is no point in doing this, since Narnia does not exist. Rilian, Eustace, Jill and Puddleglum offer up Narnia, King Caspian, the sun and Aslan himself as examples of their "real" world; but she thwarts each argument with her quiet logic. The outside world is not real, she says; it cannot be. She argues that the only real world is the underground city where they now are. The only thing that is real is that which they can see: the witch's city and all that is in it. What they are describing, she claims, is a dream and a fantasy.

[†] C. S. Lewis, *The Silver Chair*, p. 146.

Two Roads through Narnia

It is Puddleglum's courage and ultimate logic that saves them all. He stamps out the fire which has been producing the pleasant scent clouding their minds. He burns his foot, but the pain helps clear his head, and removing the mind-clouding scent helps clear the minds of the others. To Puddleglum, it's simple—her dark world strikes him as a pretty poor one. Their make-believe world "licks her real world hollow," he says. He declares he is "on Aslan's side even if there isn't any Aslan to lead it."[†] Such a statement enrages the witch, and she transforms into her true self—the worm who killed Rilian's mother. A fight to the death ensues, with the worm losing the fight (and its head).

We all face the same difficulty that these four faced when the witch was quietly convincing them that their world does not exist. We may get out of our own Silver Chairs, but once we have we must recognize what is real and what is a spell or an illusion. Otherwise we will find the Silver Chair restored, and still be sitting firmly in it.

Oddly, we can touch a tree, walk on the sidewalk in our neighborhood or enjoy a sunset, but that does not mean that only what our senses can gather is all that is real. There's more to life than what we can see, more than this pleasant darkness. We can have faith that some things which cannot be seen or touched are also real. We can choose to follow the signs that have been given us—we can believe in God. All things on Earth and Earth itself will pass, but God is forever. What can be more real?

Remember the signs and believe in the signs. Nothing else matters.

[†] C. S. Lewis, *The Silver Chair*, p. 159.

140

The Last
Battle

Well, we finally come to it. *The Chronicles of Narnia* culminates in one last tale, one last chance to meet new characters and expand our understanding of the scope of Narnia. We meet new villains, such as Shift and Ginger—and even Tash himself. And we meet some new heroes, too: King Tirian and his friends Jewel, Roonwit, Farsight the eagle—even Puzzle himself, in his own, well, puzzling way. And true to form, Lewis brings past heroes into the tale: Eustace Scrubb and Jill Pole return (and some others, too, before the tale is done).

But Lewis doesn't merely have the narrative on his mind here. He's also got some pretty significant cosmological issues to deal with from past stories. How exactly does the religion of the

Calormenes jive with Aslan and the Emperor-Beyond-the-Sea? What is the fate of those who worship Tash? For that matter, what is the fate of those who reject Aslan? Are the two questions the same? Is it heresy to suggest that both Tash and Aslan can be found in the stable? Do we all ultimately find whomever it is that we truly seek? And if Lewis was brave enough in *The Magician's Nephew* to show us how Narnia began, does he have the guts here to also show us how it ends?

The options for discussion of this book are boundless—and we simply can't tackle them all. So this time out, Jenn and I synopsize the Top Stories of all the Narnian news that's fit to print. Then George looks at the literary layers that Lewis uses to tear into (and build up) Narnia, and Kathy concludes our review of the *Chronicles* with a hard look at the stable itself.

But don't worry. The books may have ended, but the movie is coming... Just remember that films are films, not books, and have their own peculiar demands.

The Last Battle

❧ Narnia News Roundup ❦

Synopsis by Greg and Jenn Wright

TASHLAN A SCAM?

Local Ape Makes Monkey out of Donkey and Ass out of Self
From the *Daily Chronicle*

Caldron Pool – Earlier this week, eyewitness accounts had rumors of Aslan the Great's return sweeping over Narnia. Shift, the notorious ape, then set himself up as Aslan's "mouthpiece." But documents leaked to the press demonstrate that Shift may be in collusion with Calormen to promote a new myth that Tash and Aslan (or "Tashlan") are one and the same.

With the help of tradesmen from Calormen, Shift set up residence for the Great Lion at Stable Hill, where Aslan has since been making nocturnal appearances, with Shift speaking for him. "It's because I'm so wise," says Shift, "that I'm the only one Aslan is ever going to speak to. He can't be bothered talking to a lot of stupid animals."[†] At Shift's insistence, many of our talking animals have been put to work assisting Calormenes in the destruction of our friends, the trees and Dryads.

Shift has also announced that the "old idea of us being right and the Calormenes being wrong is silly." Tash, he says, is "only another name for Aslan." Ginger, the cat, and others have joined in supporting this strange alliance, in spite of Aslan's apparent change since his last confirmed appearance.

Suspicion has recently surfaced among the dwarfs that this new Aslan is nothing more than some animal sewn up in a lion skin. This rumor has not been confirmed, but government surveillance photos from Caldron Pool show that Shift and his friend Puzzle, the donkey, indeed recently came into possession of a full lion skin. Puzzle has not been seen in recent days. Unless Shift can produce both Puzzle and Tashlan simultaneously,

---

[†] C. S. Lewis, *The Last Battle*, p. 29.

something may be mucked up on Stable Hill.

NARNIA'S KING REPORTED DEAD
Monarch Loses Mind, Then Life, After Murderous Rampage
From the *Calormene HotPress*

  Cair Paravel – King Tirian of Narnia, spending a holiday at his hunting lodge not far from the eastern end of Narnia's Lantern Waste, was surprised to come upon talking beasts being used for manual labor by our fellow Calormenes, who have begun systematically chopping down Dryad trees for trade. Victims of a fit of rage, two of our innocent countrymen were murdered. Tirian and his accomplice were soon apprehended and bound to await trial. During the night, the culprits have disappeared, and are presumed dead.

  The king was not alone in his madness; in addition to Jewel, the unicorn, who shared in the slaying of mere tradesmen, Tirian was known to be in league with Roonwit the centaur, who had previously asserted that Aslan's reappearance had not been seen in the stars. But soon after Tirian's misdeed, the centaur was himself slain while attempting to stir up dissension in the vicinity of Cair Paravel. A bloody police action was necessary to put down a riot later that day. Tirian and Jewel, meanwhile, claimed to have given themselves up and sought court with Aslan, but were told that Aslan is not interested in seeing anyone personally. Witnesses at last night's fireside congress at Stable Hill heard Tirian shouting down local officials' assertions that "Aslan means neither less nor more than Tash."[†] The two culprits were then removed and bound at a distance.

  Early this morning, the king's bonds were found cut, but Shift the ape and Rishda Tarkaan report that the King was, indeed, granted audience with "Tashlan" and consumed whole. Reports of children seen with Narnia's king are thought to be lies.

[†] C. S. Lewis, *The Last Battle*, p. 32.

COLD, HARD TASH
Calormene God Makes Rare Appearance in Narnia
From *The Narnia End-Times*

Stable Hill – In the midst of unconfirmed and conflicting reports of Aslan the Great's return to Narnia, and unprecedented claims for the existence of "Tashlan," reliable witnesses are now reporting sightings of the Calormene god Tash.

In recent days, things have gone from bad to worse in Narnia. King Tirian has been deposed and is rumored to be dead. Cair Paravel has been laid waste, the majority of dwarfs have lost faith in Aslan's very existence, and vast swaths of our forests have been decimated. But new horror has come: amidst a putrid stench, moving shadow and disheartening oppression, a vast four-armed vulture-headed figure has been seen storming through the forest, heading north toward Stable Hill.

But is all lost, we wonder? Rumors that Tirian is alive may just be true. During the night, Tirian's friend Jewel, who had been held captive on trumped-up charges of murder, was also mysteriously freed; and once again a boy and girl were witnessed to be with him. Further, Shift has been unable to produce both Tashlan and his friend Puzzle simultaneously, casting further suspicions on the ape's claims about who is inhabiting Stable Hill. Has Puzzle flown the coop? And has Tash come to roost in his place? And where is the real Aslan in all of this?

CONSPIRACY UNMASKED
Shift, Ginger and Others Caught in Treasonous Pact with Invading Calormenes; Chaos Ensues
From the *Daily Chronicle*

Stable Hill – In what may be the last battle for Narnia, King Tirian last night confronted the traitorous ape, Shift, and his Calormene handlers at Stable Hill. A wild firelit battle ensued, and one by one, combatants from both sides were cast, or ran headlong into, an unknown fate in "Tashlan's" Stable.

In an event not seen since Narnia began, the first witness to

Stable Hill's resident lost the gift of speech. After being mocked by now-faithless dwarfs, Shift declared that Tashlan would make no more appearances, though single courtiers could enter and meet with him inside the stable. Ginger, sympathetic to the Tashlan regime, smugly volunteered to enter the stable and meet the hybrid god; but he exited yowling, as untranslatable as a common cat. After that, at least one Calormene was thrown dead from the door of the stable.

King Tirian, meanwhile, who appeared during this charade accompanied by two heroes of Narnia-past (Jill Pole and Eustace Scrubb), brought with him the donkey, Puzzle, missing since rumors began to surface. Sources assure us that Puzzle, like Jewel, was, indeed, rescued from the stable, having been crudely sewn into a lion skin by the scheming Shift.

Rishda Tarkaan and Shift then lost control at Stable Hill, and armed conflict broke out. Tirian, Jewel, Farsight the eagle and all true Narnians withstood more than one assault from Calormene forces. Dozens of opportunistic dwarfs rallied to the cry "Dwarfs for the Dwarfs!" and actively slaughtered combatants from both sides. Most of Narnia's talking horses were slain in the melee. One by one, the dwarfs were overcome by Calormene forces and thrown into the stable as sacrifices to Tash. They joined Shift, who had been hurled into the stable by Tirian as the battle began. Ruefully, Tirian's early success in the battle waned as Calormene reinforcements arrived. One by one, the King's companions either fell or were captured. Eustace was the first to be added to the list of human sacrifices to Tash. Jill followed Eustace not long after. Finally, Tirian fought Rishda Tarkaan himself, and forcefully took him to join the rest in the stable.

What is their fate? We do not yet know. After Tirian and Rishda disappeared, the battle soon died down. Both sides now uneasily await new developments during this brief lull in the fighting. Only one thing is clear: Aslan is not here, and never was. But everyone feels that the dawn will bring an end to this chapter of Narnia's history, and maybe an end to Narnia itself.

NEWS FROM THE OTHER SIDE
Aslan Triumphant; Tash Banished; Narnia Reborn
From the *Real Narnia News*

The Western Mountains – In a series of wholly unexpected events, Aslan has made his final victorious appearance, and all that was ever wrong has been made right.

First, the mystery of Stable Hill is resolved. Both Tash and Aslan were to be found inside, and Tash took those who belonged to him. His evil task accomplished, he slunk away at Aslan's command. The Friends of Narnia, meanwhile—the High Kings Peter and Edmund, Queen Lucy, Digory Kirke, Polly Plummer, Queen Helen and King Frank—were called by Aslan to join Eustace and Jill in this glorious triumph: this new Land of Narnia, beyond the stable door.

In a curious twist of fate, the dwarfs who passed the stable door were taken neither by Tash nor by Aslan, but by a strange darkness. As Aslan noted, the "dwarfs chose cunning instead of belief. Their prison is only in their own minds."[†]

And as hard as it may be to believe, Aslan himself opened the stable door on the Old Narnia, and brought it to a swift end. The spirits who were Narnia's stars fell from the sky; Father Time snuffed the light from the sun and the moon; and every being that ever lived in Narnia came rushing to Aslan as he stood at the door and cold and darkness descended. Each one either passed into shadow, or was called "further up and further in" to the New Land—a new land for those who served Aslan in their hearts, whether they knew they did so or not. Among Aslan's new subjects is numbered Emeth, the Calormene.

We have all journeyed through this New Narnia and beyond, in fellowship with the Heroes of Narnia, new and old, and have ascended the Western Mountains into circles of Narnia ever higher—beyond time, beyond history and beyond death.

[†] C. S. Lewis, *The Last Battle*, p. 148.

❧ Of Onions, Narnia and the *Chronicles* ❧

Literary Analysis by George Rosok

Near the end of C. S. Lewis' *The Last Battle*, Lucy and the faun Tumnus—whom she (and the rest of us) met when she first entered Narnia through the wardrobe—discuss the world through which they are walking. Lucy and her companions have followed Aslan "further up and further in" as he instructed, passing through a series of worlds that resemble Narnia. The Narnia in which they actually lived had been brought to an end at Aslan's bidding, yet each of the worlds through which they have since passed appears to be just like Narnia—only each appears more "real" than the last. Tumnus says the progression is "like an onion: except that as you continue to go in and in, each circle is larger than the last."[†]

Tumnus' words are an apt self-referential metaphor for what Lewis succeeds in doing with this last book in the Narnia series, on more levels than one.

First, his story peels the layers of Narnia away as he chronicles the events that will eventually lead to its demise; the story starts very simply, but as it progresses, the imagery and narrative become more imaginative and complex.

Second, he skillfully and imaginatively documents the end of the Narnia we know, putting the layers of the onion back together as he describes the new worlds through which the characters pass—and the imagery in the latter part of the book is the most vivid and interesting of the entire series.

Let us first examine the onion-peeling he works in getting to the heart the story. It starts with great simplicity, introducing Puzzle the donkey and his "friend" the ape, Shift. Shift is a master manipulator, convincing Puzzle to do almost any task by turning things on their head, and making it always look as if he is doing

---

[†] C. S. Lewis, *The Last Battle*, p. 180.

Puzzle a favor.

In this way, for starters, Shift persuades Puzzle to jump into Caldron Pool to retrieve a floating object. What Puzzle nearly drowns for turns out to be a lion skin. Shift convinces Puzzle to go on a long walk, regardless of Puzzle's exhaustion from his struggle in the pool. When Puzzle returns, Shift shames Puzzle into wearing the lion skin as a cloak, even though Puzzle worries that it might be disrespectful to the Great Lion, Aslan.

In the passages describing these events, Lewis writes in a simple prose. The technique is reminiscent of fables in which the characters introduce a dilemma, then go on to solve it and deliver a simple moral message. However, rather than leading to a simple resolution, *The Last Battle*'s humble beginning avalanches into the eventual elimination of an entire world. Shift, of course, has plans for Puzzle and that rough-sewn disguise—as we soon discover after we are introduced to Tirian, the current King of Narnia.

The King and his best friend Jewel are enjoying a bucolic morning at Tirian's hunting lodge. They have heard that Aslan may be back in Narnia after a long absence, and they are joyously hopeful. But the Centaur, Roonwit, arrives and dispels that notion, warning that the stars tell of no visit from Aslan. At nearly the same time, a Dryad appears, crying out that trees are being murdered—and then she collapses, her own tree apparently also felled.

The tone of Lewis' prose grows more complex as the causes behind these tragedies unfold. Tirian and Jewel are eager to be off to investigate and prosecute those responsible. Roonwit counsels that Tirian should wait, but Tirian sends Roonwit to Cair Paravel for reinforcements while he and Jewel go off to the forests. They discover that the felled trees are to be sold to Calormenes and that talking animals are aiding in this endeavor. Even worse, the animals claim that their work is at Aslan's command. Tirian and Jewel decide they must go on and "take the adventure that comes to us."[†] They are determined to do this even though they are crestfallen over the possibility that all that they and their ancestors have believed about Aslan all these years may not be true.

At this point Lewis' prose even becomes omniscient. The narrator informs us that Tirian "did not see at the moment how foolish it was for [him and Jewel] to go on alone... But much evil came of their rashness in the end."[‡] And much evil did result; but did their actions change the outcome? Not as far as we can see, because Roonwit would soon enough be killed even before he reached Cair Paravel—and Cair Paravel itself, we learn later, had already been overrun by Calormenes, its occupants killed or on the run. So at this point Tirian and Jewel are already on a path leading to Narnia's demise—going "further up and further in" through the events that will lead to destruction, powerless to change the outcome, though they will fight with every fiber of their beings in the attempt to save Narnia. So we must trust that Lewis' narration at this point *is* omniscient. The story itself does not convince us that what the narrator tells us is true; instead, we must take the narrator at his word.

But events are indeed unraveling Narnia. Jill and Eustace arrive to help Tirian and Jewel, who have turned themselves over to the Calormenes, having rashly murdered two of their soldiers. Together, the party soon confirms that the "Aslan" who has appeared is the donkey Puzzle, dressed in a lion suit and acting as the puppet of Shift who, with the help of the Calormenes, wishes to impose his avaricious whims and desires on credulous Narnians. Jill manages to capture the masquerading donkey—or rather release him, since Puzzle is more than eager to stop the ruse.

The situation continues to unravel as a succession of plans and hopes comes to naught. Our protagonists are helpless, and each of them is forced into the stable where they expect to meet

---

[†] C. S. Lewis, *The Last Battle*, p. 20.
[‡] Ibid.

their demise either by the Calormene soldier hiding there or by the Calormene god, Tash, who has come into Narnia—unwittingly called there by Rishda Tarkaan. Once inside, though, Tirian, who is last to enter, is surprised to see that he is in another world lit by an early summer sun; and he is welcomed by all the "Friends of Narnia"—Digory, Polly, Peter, Edmund, Lucy, Eustace and Jill. And at this juncture, Lewis' prose takes an even stranger turn, as the battle which still rages outside the stable—and the fate of Tirian's other friends—is wholly forgotten in favor of chuckles, high language and diversions with dwarfs.

Susan is not there, however. The one purely negative critique I have of this story concerns the narrator's comments regarding Susan. I concede that I was somewhat perplexed earlier in the story when the "Friends of Narnia" were short a member. In an odd aside at this point, Lewis' story takes time to explain that Susan is no longer a friend of Narnia. The true "friends" explain to Tirian (and to us) that Susan no longer remembers her adventures in Narnia as having actually occurred. Jill says, "She's interested in nothing nowadays except nylons and lipstick and invitations. She always was a jolly sight too keen on being grown-up."[†] This aside seems to serve little purpose in the story. It is also a weak mini-critique of how we turn our backs on childhood and our core values as we grow older. Yet what makes this interlude even possible is the increasingly complex narrative layers that Lewis employs.

But let's get back to the situation in which Tirian now finds himself. He and all the Friends of Narnia are clean and in fresh new clothes. Aslan soon greets them, but they stand witness as Aslan directs the end of Narnia.

Lewis' imagery now becomes exceptionally interesting. A giant (Father Time from *The Silver Chair*) rises up and blows his horn. The stars fall from the sky—but remember, in Narnia stars are living beings. The beings fall from the sky and stand among the Friends, still glowing, lighting the landscape. Then all the

---

[†] C. S. Lewis, *The Last Battle*, p. 135.

creatures of that world are called and come racing toward them as Aslan stands at the door, casting a great shadow to his left. To his right is entry into the new world. As the creatures approach him, those who are terrified or angry run to Aslan's left into darkness, never to be seen again. The others, who are joyful (if perhaps also fearful of Aslan), move to Aslan's right and into the new world.

The powerful imagery continues as a flood rises up that covers all the land. The sun and the moon come up one after the other, and the sun engulfs the moon. Then, at Aslan's command, the giant throws his horn into the sea and squeezes the sun until there is total darkness. Everything becomes frozen; Aslan commands Peter to close the door—and at that the Friends and their companions believe Narnia is no more. Naturally, they grieve, Lucy in particular. And here the first phase of Lewis' narrative layering concludes. All of the layers of the Narnia we have known before have been exposed.

But Aslan is quite happy and calls over his shoulder as he races away, "Come further in! Come further up!"[†] Lewis is about to put the layers back together again in his second narrative phase.

As the Friends and company go further in, they (and we) meet up with many characters from past Narnian adventures. They all gradually begin to notice how this new world looks strikingly familiar—and they realize that this world is just like Narnia, only "more like the real thing."[‡]

They continue into this new world, where Lewis paints a wonderful image of all of them diving into Caldron Pool and swimming up the waterfall to another land—which is an even *more* real Narnia. After emerging, they run all the way to the West Mountains where they climb the hill (now mountain) on top of which is the garden that Digory had entered to retrieve the apple in *The Magician's Nephew*. There they find that they are not simply in a garden but in another entire world—another, grander

---

[†] C. S. Lewis, *The Last Battle*, p. 158.

[‡] Ibid., p. 169.

Narnia that is yet again more real than all the previous Narnias.

So Lewis and his characters add layers to the onion of the "real" Narnia for us, and in the end we have discovered an entirely new, vast and grand Ideal Narnia to inhabit—one that will never be subject to Jadis, Miraz, Shift or the like.

Through his imagery and narrative style, Lewis provides an example we all can follow. We also can find ways to peel the old, dead layers of our lives away and add new ones to find a more real and greater existence.

How often do we find ourselves consumed in our own routine, acting out an extended version of muscle-memory rather than acknowledging that what we do actually affects our lives and the lives of others? How much more could we accomplish by also going further up and further in?

One of my current favorite musicians is a young Australian artist named Ben Lee. The title song of his latest album is "Awake is the New Sleep." In this song he cheerfully admonishes all of us who are holding back, just going through the motions, to "wake up and just do it." Written half a century apart, similar advice from both Lewis and Lee is effective counsel for us all.

"Come further in! Come further up!"

"Wake up and just do it!"

❧ The Stable-ity of Narnia ❧

Spiritual Commentary by Kathy Bledsoe

*After this I looked, and there before me was a door
standing open in heaven...* —Revelation 4:1

There is a rather trite saying going around garden stores
these days. It can be found on placards made to hang in sheds or
atop metal flowerbed stakes or even on magnets that are sure to
be added to refrigerator doors already groaning from the weight of
collected "wisdom," cherished family pictures and coupons for cat
food. The sentiment?

Life Began in a Garden.

In *The Last Battle*, C. S. Lewis presents us with a child-
friendly (if sometimes gruesome) version of the Bible's book of
Revelation. And in this version, the focal point is not a really a
garden, but a stable. This does not refute the Biblical truth of life
beginning in the Garden of Eden, of course, but instead opens up
the larger question of which life is most worth pursuing—eternal
life with Aslan in his world, or eternal destruction and separation
from Aslan. Just as Aslan uses the stable as the doorway of
decision into the real Narnia, God used a stable as the foundation
of decision for mankind—the beginning of the end, if you will.

The Bible tells us that Eden originally became off-limits
because of the sin committed there by Adam and Eve, which
doomed humanity to eternal destruction. However, in an
astounding display of love and mercy, God chose a Plan B—the
birth of Jesus in a lowly, smelly stable—as the beginning of the
story of salvation. According to that story, all who believe in and
call on the name of the One born in the stable will be saved and
have life forever with God in Heaven.

With pure genius, Lewis also presents the idea that life
(eternal life—the only life that matters) begins in a stable, and
thus the stable door represents passage from the "shadow of

Narnia" into "Aslan's real world." The titular Last Battle is not the physical fighting between the Narnians and the Calormenes (which is a very limited part of the story) so much as the individual's spiritual battle of choice: the stable of salvation or the stable of destruction. The irony is that both buildings are really one and the same, and Lewis uses his characters well to prove this point.

Of foremost import is the fact that Lewis chooses to capitalize the word "stable." This is a device he uses throughout his writing, both fiction and non-fiction, when he wants the reader to take notice and get a point. It is no accident that Shift, the ape, creates an Anti-Aslan with a lion skin on Puzzle, the donkey, and houses him in a Stable.

Each character or group of characters subsequently represents a response to the invitation to enter the Stable of Eternal Life. The chosen response determines the final destination of the individual—to dwell with Aslan forever or to become fodder for Tash.

First we must deal with Shift. The Apostle Peter has two very clear warnings that pertain to who Shift is and what he is doing here:

> *Be self-controlled and alert. Your enemy the devil prowls around like a roaring lion looking for someone to devour.*   *—1 Peter 5:8*

> *... there will be false teachers among you. They will secretly introduce destructive heresies, even denying the sovereign Lord who bought them— bringing swift destruction on themselves.*   *—2 Peter 2:1*

The ape is one who knows who Aslan is but defiantly refuses to bow before him. He creates an Anti-Aslan, but in truth is the Anti-Christ himself. He becomes the lord and "mouthpiece of Aslan," claiming that he is "so wise that [he is] the only one Aslan is ever going to speak to." Shift invents "Tashlan" and claims that Tash and Aslan are one and the same. Many Narnians buy into the ape's subterfuge, but some refuse to believe the blasphemy and are persecuted, imprisoned, even sacrificed for refusing to worship Tashlan and listen to Shift.

In our own post-modern, similarly "enlightened" world, Satan's most effective weapon has been the promotion of tolerance to undermine the path to salvation. These are some of Satan's lies:

- Christians are no different from Buddhists, Muslims, Hindus, etc.

- Christ is just another man, a great prophet of history, and not the "name under heaven given to men by which [they] must be saved."[†]

- It is a silly thing to claim that the path to salvation is narrow and difficult, and must be chosen. Wouldn't Christ want everyone to be saved without such requirements? How can modern and enlightened people believe that God, who claims to be love, consigns those who do not choose Christ to eternal death?

- Christianity is an intolerant religion whose claims must be suppressed and refuted.

Shift does not accept the salvation of the Stable but creates his own religion to replace it, one designed very much along the lines of our own contemporary objections. He is an ape who wants to be a man, and misuses a good thing to deceive believers and lure them into apostasy just as Satan today tempts us to give in to the call of the world.

Puzzle, however, is an Ass: one who has enough knowledge to know there is a difference between good and evil, but one who has not developed that knowledge into a faith that can save him from being used and manipulated. He knows *of* Aslan, but has no personal experience with him. He is the perfect picture of the

---

[†] Acts 4:12.

person who believes there is a God but has not bothered to move beyond that declaration. This type of believer, one that Jesus classifies as "lukewarm,"[†] is in awe and fear of God's power to exact retribution for wrongs committed, but has no knowledge of the power of God's love and His desire to save. The Stable is just a place in which to hide or feel confined. The door of the Stable represents only a path that must be taken—knowing full well that an awful judgment is all that is deserved and all that waits on the other side. Puzzle's faith is really born when he finally meets Aslan face-to-face, and he is saved as one "snatched from the fire."[‡]

King Tirian and his friend the unicorn are both "jewels" in the rough: believers whose relationship with Aslan is not strong enough to give them the "peace of God, that transcends all understanding"[§] when conflicting reports come to them. Instead of listening to the wisdom of Roonwit, the Centaur prophet, they easily fall prey to confusion and in doing so act rashly. If they knew Aslan well, they would know him by his attributes and not just by the description, "not a tame lion." This phrase, repeated often within a few pages,[*] leads them to ignore wise counsel and to act in anger and in their own power, bringing them to commit the sin of murdering two Calormenes for beating a Narnian talking Horse—just as the biblical Moses killed an Egyptian for beating a Hebrew slave.

Since they really do not know whom they worship or why, though they long for Aslan—he has simply become a "great" lion of the past—Tirian and Jewel are easily duped into the despair that comes from discovering that the truth they thought they understood is not the truth at all. This is very much like the believer of today, one who decides that God really intends to take a "hands off" approach and leaves it up to each of us to make

---

[†] Revelation 3:16.
[‡] See Jude 1:23.
[§] Philippians 4:7.
[*] See C. S. Lewis, *The Last Battle*, p. 16ff.

decisions and run our own lives. Unfortunately, the danger is that "much evil [comes] of their rashness in the end,"[†] and we have witnessed throughout history the horrors done in the name of Christ by Christians who believe they must take God's business into their own hands.

The blessing is that Tirian and Jewel do come to understand who Aslan really is—through (not in spite of) the trials they have brought upon themselves and the errors they have committed. This offers to all believers the hope of complete restoration (despite all the wrong turns along the way) and the joy of hearing Christ say, "Well done, good and faithful servant,"[‡] just as Aslan says to King Tirian. The walk of faith is a life-long process, not an overnight *fait accompli*.

Tirian discovers that when a person gets to his lowest point and finally calls on the name of Aslan, the Great Emperor-Beyond-the-Sea responds to the prayer of faith—and acts. The result isn't always what was expected; but then comes true understanding of the phrase, "not a tame lion." Aslan cannot be manipulated or controlled. Aslan does not act in whimsical and arbitrary ways. Aslan can be trusted to remain true to his character and to be consistent in word and action. Aslan does not change.[§]

What Tirian's prayer does is bring Jill Pole and Eustace Scrubb back into Narnia. These two characters are the last of the children from the first six books who are young enough to return to Narnia. They have a firm knowledge of Aslan, and an unwavering faith in him. These are the strengths around which King Tirian and the remaining true Narnians rally. The children's appearance brings renewed faith to Tirian, and he finds the power within himself to boldly stand up to the lie that has been perpetrated by Shift.

Jill and Eustace embody God's intention that a primary

[†] C. S. Lewis, *The Last Battle*, p. 20.
[‡] Matthew 25:21, 23.
[§] Compare with the description of God in James 1:17.

purpose of a believer's life is to encourage those whose faith may be faltering. Ask any believer today and he will surely have at least one story of a time in his life when he thought he had hit rock bottom and there was no further hope. His testimony will be that other believers "found" him, encouraged him and lifted him back to living faith. It doesn't necessarily mean that the problem was removed, only that strength was given to remain steadfast and, often, to come through the difficulty stronger in Christ than ever before.

Thanks to the children, Tirian and Jewel (though dreading the dark portal of the Stable and what may lie beyond) have the courage of faith to hope that it "may be... the door to Aslan's country"[†]—and find that this is indeed the case. Still, Tirian and all the rest went through that Stable door with imperfect knowledge, acting on faith that they would never be alone.

But finally, we must address the dwarfs' plight, for they are perhaps the characters most to be pitied and mourned. In *The Great Divorce* Lewis says, "Every state of mind, left to itself, every shutting up of the creature within the dungeon of its own mind—is, in the end, Hell."[‡] The dwarfs of *The Last Battle* epitomize this type of hell. Aslan has been absent from Narnia for so long that the dwarfs, if not complete atheists, are at least agnostic. They feel sorely abused for having been fooled by a dressed-up donkey, and agree with Griffle, who says, "I've heard as much about Aslan as I want to for the rest of my life."[§]

When the dwarfs enter the same Stable as all of the other characters, and when Truth stands embodied in Aslan, they cannot see him. At Lucy's behest, Aslan prepares a wonderful banquet for the dwarfs—but their incomprehensible perception is that they are eating straw in a stinking stable. "You see," says Aslan, "they will not let us help them. They have chosen cunning instead of belief. Their prison is only in their own minds, yet they are in that

---

[†] C. S. Lewis, *The Last Battle*, p. 128.
[‡] C. S. Lewis, *The Great Divorce*, p. 69.
[§] C. S. Lewis, *The Last Battle*, p. 71.

prison; and so afraid of being taken in that they cannot be taken out."[†]

Wayne Martindale, in his book *Beyond the Shadowlands: C. S. Lewis on Heaven & Hell*, warns, "The Dwarfs' case is a warning that hypocrites provide agnostics with a rationalization for not believing anything. A pretender once seen through is a more powerful weapon in Satan's arsenal than an outright atheist."[‡] An atheist is, after all, actually in the habit of believing in something—a habit that can be turned in a different direction. C. S. Lewis provides himself as a case in point.

But what happens to Shift, Ginger the Cat and Rishda Tarkaan? None of the three believe in anything supernatural. They create their own god, Tashlan, to manipulate those vulnerable and gullible beings around them in order to assume power. The Tash in whom he does not believe consumes Shift. Ginger loses his sanity. Rishda is carried off by a very real "non-existent" being. In the end, we can only assume that the three finally believe that Tash, at least, is real!

Agnostics, though, as we see with the dwarfs, are very difficult to persuade to believe in anything. "Once bitten, twice shy" is an extremely difficult philosophy to break down. The agnostic dwarfs cannot see nor comprehend the glory of the Stable, and so are consigned forever to the Hell of their own minds. Significantly, this seems no better a fate than that which awaits those who pass into Aslan's shadow.

The Stable of *The Last Battle* forces each character to confront what he believes and to act accordingly. The door leads either into the real Narnia (which will exist for all eternity) or back into the "shadowland" Narnia, which is swallowed up into oblivion.

The Stable in Bethlehem on that cold, starry night two thousand years ago welcomed a baby who would transform the

---

[†] C. S. Lewis, *The Last Battle*, p. 148.

[‡] Wayne Martindale, *Beyond the Shadowlands: C. S. Lewis on Heaven & Hell*, p. 194.

meaning of life. When we understand the beauty of that child, and the sweet smell of Jesus' sacrifice rising to Heaven from the cross, we have truly left the concept of the lowly and stinking stable behind, and are ready to accept the invitation to "Come further up, further in!"

Glossary of Obscure Terms

C. S. Lewis was a not merely a musty old scholar. He was also a well-read man, and the language he uses in *The Chronicles of Narnia* reflects both his voracious literary appetite and his fascination for archaic (even dead) languages. As a result, a great number of the terms that Lewis employs in these stories can be literally unfathomable—without some help.

In addition, many of the words he uses carry a sense uniquely tied to England, or to specific settings and periods; and though we may be familiar enough with England—or London, or a general history of the First World War—we may still need some help divining the exact word-sense that Lewis was after: because Lewis was not just familiar with these things, he was British, he knew London and he lived through the First World War.

This Glossary of Obscure Terms is intended to help readers wade through some of Lewis' more cryptic usage. We have not included definitions, however, for words you are likely to find in a garden-variety dictionary. These are just the most choice humdingers, taken from all seven books in the *Chronicles* and arranged alphabetically.

Adam and Eve. The names given by the Bible to the first man and woman. In the context of the *Chronicles*, "Son of Adam" and "Daughter of Eve" mean "beings of human origin."

Adept. A psychic operator, similar to a medium; but whereas a medium passively channels spirits, an adept actively controls them.

Air-raids. Bombing missions. During the early years of World War II, Germany frequently sent squadrons of bombers to lay waste to industrial and urban districts of England. (The Allies, of course, sent similar missions to Germany, and did so more frequently after the Luftwaffe lost air supremacy in Europe.)

Apartments. Rooms within a dwelling space. In America, we'd just say "apartment," probably.

Apothegm. A short pithy quote, like an aphorism, epigram or proverb. Need some more definitions now?

August. Not the month. This is an adjective indicating an aspect of character that induces awe or veneration.

Bacchus. The Roman name for the mythological god of wine. Narnia is an interesting place...

Baccy. That's tobacco. Remember, Tolkien put tobacco in Middle-earth, too, though he later tried to get away with calling it "pipe-weed." The pleasures of nicotine and lung cancer are apparently common to all worlds.

Bagged. Stolen. In origin, from poaching (illegal hunting), in which the meat was hidden in bags.

Bally. Used kind of as a substitute for the stronger "bloody." Think of a mild term that a polite child might use instead of an expletive.

Balustrade. Okay, this is kind of interesting, because basically we're just talking about a railing. But it's called a "balustrade" because the rail is mounted on "balusters," or pillars of a sort, in order to form a protective barrier along a parapet or stairwell. So we've all seen balustrades but probably never called them that.

Battened. When I pretended to be on a storm-tossed sea as a child, I had no idea what I meant when I shouted, "Batten down the hatches!" It was just the thing you were supposed to do. But the idea is that "battening"—cotton wadding or other fabric—would be used to seal the hatches so that seawater would not flood the lower decks.

Below the Belt. A term from the days when "being a good sport" meant something. The idea here is that it used to be considered poor sportsmanship to hit a man in his private parts. It hurts.

Bezzling. Embezzling, of course. Taking money that's only yours to count.

Billy-oh. Archaic British slang for "a whole bunch."

Blue-bottle. A particular type of housefly.

Boarding School. Sure, we all know this is a type of school you go to live at. But why "boarding"? Because "board" is what we now refer to as "meals." A "boarding house," in which many of our grandparents and great-grandparents lived in the years following the Great Depression, offered both "room" and "board" for the price of rent.

Boatswain. The crewmember in charge of keeping the boat's deck ship-shape. Heh heh. In much of sea-going jargon, this is shortened to "bos'n" or "bosun."

Bobance. A brag or boast. Like, "I know what 'bosun' means. So there!"

Boggle. Hobgoblin or bogie.

Boon. A granted request.

Bottom. This is a reference to Shakespeare's *A Midsummer Night's Dream*, which featured a fool named Bottom.

Bow-window. A curving window case set out from the wall, allowing a view down each direction of the exterior. Also "bay window."

Brick. A helpful, reliable person. Solid, dependable.

Buskins. Soft, slipper-like leather shoes.

Butcher's Boy. A young man or boy employed to assist in a butcher's shop with various tasks, including the task of deliveries.

Camphor. The active ingredient in mothballs. It carries a distinctive odor (one that moths apparently dislike).

Canny. Careful and shrewd. Not really the opposite of "uncanny."

Cantrip. A trick.

Caraways. Cakes or sweetmeats flavored with caraway seed.

Carbuncle. In medical parlance, this is a boil resulting from an infected hair follicle, one red and swollen. In this context, however, it's the jewel talked about in the King James Bible (see Exodus 39:10, for instance): a red gem, generally thought to be garnet.

Career. A full-speed run.

Glossary

Carracks. Square-rigged, multi-masted ocean-going vessels. Magellan circumnavigated the earth in a carrack.

Cat-a-mountains. Mountain lions. Sometimes shortened to "catamounts."

Catches. As the American Heritage Dictionary would have it, these are "canonic, often rhythmically intricate compositions for three or more voices, popular especially in the 17th and 18th centuries." I'll just have to take their word for it.

Chaplet. A wreath worn on the head.

Charger. A swift horse trained for use in the cavalry.

Chatelaine. The lady of a castle.

Christian Name. The name that comes before the family name: your first name. It came to be called the "Christian" name because of the once-universal Western practice of infant baptism, during which the baby was officially christened with its given name.

Christmas. As we see later in the story, a season of giving rather than the holiday with religious underpinnings which we practice in our world (the "Christ-Mass").

Clothes. Now, I have to admit that the first two times I read *The Voyage of the* Dawn Treader, I thought the point Lewis was making was that the Scrubbs were very neat and tidy people—who, you know, unlike me, didn't leave a bunch of laundry scattered all over the room, including on the bed. But what Lewis means by "very few clothes on the beds" is that the Scrubbs believed in sleeping more cold than warm; that is, the beds didn't have many blankets on them. Am I a little slow in the uptake, or what?

Cob. According the American Heritage Dictionary, a "thickset, stocky, short-legged horse." Bree is once again making a slighting reference to other, less impressive horses. Ahem.

Cock-a-leekie. Aha. Now, I actually had some of this the last time I was in Scotland. It's a soup made from chicken and leeks. There now, that was easy, wasn't it?

Cock-shies. A game in which you toss a ball (or large rock, apparently) at another object in order to knock it off its perch.

Cogs. Single-masted trading ships; typical in the thirteenth and fourteenth centuries of our world.

Coil. Noise and confusion; fuss and ruckus.

Coiner. An alchemist, one able to turn lead to gold: to mint one's own coin. In this context, a magician of sorts.

Comfits. Seeds, nuts or bits of fruit coated with sugar. There. That sounds better, doesn't it?

Coronets. Light crowns, mere circlets almost. My dad played a cornet, incidentally. Not only spelled differently, it's like a trumpet and doesn't fit very comfortably on one's head. Not that I ever tried, mind you.

Cricket-bat. Okay, it's kind of odd to be discussing the game of cricket in connection to Narnia. But this is a reference to the revered British game of bat-and-ball, not a reference to a device designed to injure certain insects.

Crockery. Earthenware plates, bowls and so on. A step up from primitive wooden stuff, but still pretty rustic and certainly not fine china or the great melanine stuff we use today.

Crumpets. Apparently, it's very British to burst out with something like "Crabs and crumpets!" instead of out-and-out cursing. But for the record, a crumpet is essentially what Americans call an "English Muffin." Only better. And actually English.

Curds. Now, this is really strange, but in societies of the past, curdled dairy product was a delicacy. And while cottage cheese is still with us, it's hardly considered the food of royalty.

Dais. Okay, the big deal here is not what the word itself means. It's a raised platform. The question is, how do you pronounce it? The answer: "day-iss."

Dark Lantern. A lantern with a single closeable opening, rather than open all around. Figures prominently in Poe's "The Tell-tale Heart."

Dastard. Not a misspelling. Think "dastardly." A coward.

Devices. Symbols. Heraldry was the art of conveying—in "devices" upon shields, banners and so on—a knight's heritage.

Downs. Rolling hills. It really sounds funny to say "up here in the downs," as Bree does, doesn't it?

Drains, The. The plumbing in London's early row houses was notoriously clogged, and the resulting seepage was credited with the spread of typhus. The explanation Polly's father offers about the vacant home, then, is that it was closed for health reasons.

Dripping. Grease or fat. Back when we all ate less healthily, it was quite common to leave the drippings from fried bacon, for instance, in the bottom of the pan. The liquid fat would solidify as it cooled and would liquefy again when reheated. Other food (such as fish) would then be fried in the drippings.

Dromonds. Speedy Byzantine sailing galleys, specifically designed for war.

Dumb. Without the ability to speak. This is not intended as an insult. Okay, maybe it is, in this context.

Dunce's Caps. Back when teachers were allowed to insult and intimidate their students, slow learners might be made to wear a tall, cone-shaped paper hat to indicate that they were "dunces," or stupid (dense in the head).

Efreets. A branch of the Jinn.

Electric Torch. A two-dollar word for "flashlight." Of course, we easily forget than fifty or so years ago a flashlight was a much bigger deal than it is now.

Estres. A Middle-English word meaning "inner rooms." King Lune is proposing a full tour of the castle, not just the battlements.

Ettins. Giants. In Tolkien's Middle-earth, the Ettenmoors are where the giant stone-trolls are found. North of Narnia, the Ettinsmoor is where the stone-tossing giants reside.

Examination. A test, not a medical inspection, or anything of that sort.

Fast. Secure. Whew!

Father Christmas. A European (but mostly British) version of Santa Claus.

Faugh! An exclamation of disgust. The short form, apparently, of an Irish war cry meaning "clear the way."

Firkin. A type of cask, most frequently used to store ale. Casks

Glossary

were formed of staves, like barrels, but were much smaller. A firkin generally held nine gallons, or about a quarter barrel.

Flannel. Not so many years ago, "flannel" by definition meant "wool." These days, we don't wear so much wool, and flannel (almost by definition) means "cotton," which is quite comfortable. Unlined wool flannel, by contrast, tends to be pretty scratchy stuff to wear.

Fledge. To grow a covering of feathers, which is what Strawberry, in a way, does.

Foal. Since Bree is talking here, he's calling Shasta "young." Of course, there's a pun there, too, with "fool."

Football. Everywhere but America, this means soccer. So I suppose that's the case in Narnia, too!

Fricasseed. Cut into small pieces and made into a stew called a "fricassee." We can just guess how that darn stew got its name. (From the French word for "fry and break up," more or less.)

Frowsty. Stale.

Galleon. That's galleon, not gallon. One's a big ship, the other's a big measure of liquid.

Gasometer. Before gas was piped directly to homes, it was stored in a central location in huge tanks. These were called gasometers. In science, gasometers are still used to capture gas and then, floating in a tank of water, used to measure the weight of the gas pumped into the drum. I actually used one of these beasties back in the dark ages, before neat little electronic spirometers were invented.

Gay. Just happy. My, wasn't life simpler fifty years ago?

Ginger Beer. A non-alcoholic carbonated refreshment made from lime and ginger root. The carbonation is derived from yeast. Similar to Root Beer.

Girdle. A wide sash worn around the waist. Used to "gird up the loins," so to speak, if you've ever read the King James version of the Old Testament. I think this was probably done to prevent hernias during heavy exertion!

Grain Elevators. I presume that this will be confusing for some people. Maybe not. But these are silos (tall, usually cylindrical structures used to store grain) that are outfitted with some mechanical means of getting the grain in and out. You really can't ride a grain elevator. Much.

Hansom. A particular type of horse-drawn taxi in which the driver sat high up behind the cab. These are still in use today as a novelty.

Hastilude. A contest of arms.

Hols. Okay, it'd be easy enough to say "holidays" and let it go at that. But it's probably worth pointing out that the British "holiday" is synonymous with the Yank "vacation." So there's a little more than just casual jargon working here. And the fact that the kids say "hols" instead of "holidays" tells the (British) reader that these kids are pretty posh.

Homely. Not "a touch on the ugly side," but just plain "home-like."

Hooters. Owls. *Owls.*

How. A mound raised over a burial site, with tunnels bisecting the mound for access to the venerated site. If you're ever in Scotland, you can visit an ancient How up in the Orkney Islands.

Glossary

Hyaline. Transparent, like gossamer. The wings of a dragonfly, for instance, are said to be hyaline.

"I'd as lief..." "I'd willingly..."

Jade. A nagging, mean-spirited or shrewish woman.

Jiggered. To be confused or confounded; from archaic British. Perhaps, to be lost or taken advantage of in a back alley.

Jinn. Plural; synonymous with "genies."

Joint. Wow. Can this just get out of hand, or what? This means "piece of meat," specifically one with the bone in. Like leg of lamb, you know?

Kirtle. Fancy (and archaic) word for "dress," pretty much. It'd be best not to confuse this with "girdle," though, because it'd be pretty funny to see some lady riding a horse in nothing but a green girdle.

Leads. Flat-roofed areas of a castle, covered in sheets of lead.

Lemon-squash. The British version of lemonade. But it's really not much like lemonade. I think they must crush the rind, too. But then, I've only had the bottled stuff. Not terribly pleasant, I must say. But we're pretty spoiled these days.

Lilith. The apocryphal and demonic first wife of Adam.

Litter. A small platform mounted on poles that allow it to be carried; it also allows one or more people to ride and be carried, and that's the point here. Special people (or people who just think they're special, and therefore employ slaves) are carried on litters.

Lodge a Disposition. Sounds kind of like fancy language for "get something stuck in your throat." It's actually fancy language for "make a complaint."

Lover. Okay. Times change. In Lewis' day, lovers were simply people who were rather fond of each other. In this context, we don't need go any further than that (neither did Susan and Rabadash).

Made Love. Okay, hasn't this all just been a huge exercise in how drastically our language has changed? Today this means, basically, "had sex." Here it means nothing of the sort. It simply means "buttered up."

Malapert. An impudent, disrespectful person. Any time a word begins with "mal," it means something bad.

Manikin. Literally, "little man." Disrespect is meant in this usage.

Marry. An exclamation that has nothing to do with being married. Used a lot in Shakespeare, for instance.

Mazer. A large drinking bowl, probably wooden.

Mill-race. The stream of water that moves a water wheel, the source of hydraulic energy used for centuries to drive milling operations.

Miscarry. Go awry. Tirian is not suggesting that he's pregnant; he's suggesting that his plans might fail.

Moke. Just an archaic term for "donkey."

Monomachy. Single combat, usually in the form of a duel.

Moor. On the one hand, a Moor is a person of Arabic descent. But that's not what we're talking about here. A moor, in this context (according to the American Heritage Dictionary), is a "broad area of open land, often high but poorly drained, with patches of heath and peat bogs." I know, I know: How does that distinguish a moor from most of the rest of the British Isles? But there ya go.

Moth-ball. A manufactured product used to repel moths. Stored clothing (particularly woolens and furs) is susceptible to damage from moths.

Muffler. A heavy scarf. Much easier to wear and far less heavy than car parts (though probably not as warm).

Mutton. Not merely sheep's meat, but the meat of a fully grown and usually tough sheep. A poor meat for poor folks, known for its particularly strong, greasy smell.

Nosegay. You can kind of see, I think, how the word "bouquet" became more common, can't you?

Old Cove. A fairly common British euphemism for an elderly person, much like "old bat." Usually intended as an insult.

Orbo. A large lute. Not very helpful? Okay, I'll also tell you that the lute was a forerunner of the mandolin. So since the mandolin is like a small violinish (but strummed and picked) guitar, the orbo must have been a violinish guitar.

Orknies. Possibly related to Tolkien's "orcs," or goblins of some type.

Pajock. Peacock, but used as term of contempt.

Panniers. Originally, these were large bread baskets slung onto pack animals. Today, these are fabric bags used in balanced pairs on bicycles and so forth. In the context of this story, these were probably general-use baskets or bags that Shift would sling across Puzzle's back.

Pantomime. Ordinarily we associate this with something like what you do when you play charades. You know, no talking, just gestures and motions. But properly speaking, that's more "mime" than "pantomime." And in the period that Lewis is writing about, the word really just meant "acting," more or less—and specifically, a fairy-tale type of entertainment for kids at Christmastime. My British friend Helen says, "The difficult bit for Americans to understand is that the principal boy is played by a female actor—a pantomime dame played by a man in drag!"

Pasty. Everyone in Britain knows that a pasty is a type of baked meat pie, rather like a small calzone (only not Italian, and certainly not spicy). They're rather good, though, particularly with peas and a pint of cider. I should know. Pronounced "pass-tee."

Pavender. Okay, this word has actually been used a lot in these books. It's a type of fish. Just don't ask me what type—because I don't know!

Pawn. To exchange personal property for money as a secured loan. A pawn shop sells unclaimed pawned goods. Glenn Miller famously pawned his trombone several times before making good.

Pax. Latin for "peace." Children today might say "truce" or "time out."

Pedlars. British variant of "peddlers," or traveling salesmen.

Physic. Now, in some of Lewis' books (like *Prince Caspian*), this word means "doctor." In others, it most likely means "medicine." What it doesn't mean, in any case, is "physics," the science, only with the "s" left off.

Pillar-box. A type of mailbox or postbox fashioned by cutting a slot in a metal cylinder or hollow pillar.

Plashing. No, there's no "s" missing there. To plash is to make a light splashing sound.

Poltroon. A salt's term for "coward."

Pomely. Dappled, or spotted.

Pomona. A wood-nymph known for her cultivation of fruit. She is the principal character of a fable recorded by Bulfinch.

Poop. A section of the deck of a ship; specifically, a weather deck at the stern (back). So a "feast on the poop" isn't what it sounds like at first. Think context!

Possets. Ooh, ouch. These are spiced drinks made from sweetened milk mixed with wine or other alcoholic beverages, which curdles the milk. Yep. Sounds great!

Postern. Most fortified cities naturally had large gates. That's how you'd get big things in, like Trojan horses and such. Sort of. But cities (and castles) also had posterns: small, stout doors just big enough for people to get in and out of. A postern figures prominently in the battle at Helm's Deep in Tolkien's *The Two Towers*.

Posts. Messages, or letters. It's been a long time since Americans have used that word in that way; but a "Post Office" is still where you "post" letters.

Punt. A type of small boat.

Puttees. Cloths wrapped around the pantlegs from ankle to knee. Like with gaiters, the point is to keep water and debris from easily getting into your boots.

Quay. A weird term for "wharf." Pronounced "key." Useful when playing Scrabble. (Also see "Jinn"!)

Queer. Simply "odd" in this context.

Rather! A British exclamation indicating enthusiastic (and sometimes sarcastic) agreement. Similar to "Sure thing!" or "I suppose!"

Recorder. Not a primitive MP3 maker, but a musical instrument of the whistle family.

Reef. To bring in the sails and lash them down. A severe wind could shred the canvas, which would be very, very bad.

Rive. To tear apart. "Riven" means "torn apart."

Road-drill. A loud machine for breaking concrete, like a jackhammer. The point here is "loud." Really loud.

Rude. Today, we almost universally use this term to mean, "Behaving as a cable news talk show host." Lewis, however, uses the term to mean "rough" or "crude" (and no, he doesn't use "crude" to describes those same cable personalities, either—though perhaps he would if he were alive today).

Rum Go. Strange luck. In British vernacular, "rum" generally means "odd" or "bad."

Saffron. A spice of yellow-orange color, harvested from crocus blossoms. The spice is also used as a dye.

Sal Volatile. Smelling salts. Used to revive the fainted.

Sapient. Wise. This is worth commenting on in this context since the human species is called "homo sapiens," which means "wise man." Hence, the Calormene is using this term with extreme irony in addressing Shift, who is, after all, merely an ape.

School Baths. Swimming pools. Swimming pools!

Scullery. The nasty, smelly part of the kitchen where the dishes are cleaned. So this is where all the refuse piles up. Not a nice thing in big old castles filled with giants.

Scullions. The poor unlucky servants who work in the scullery.

Glossary

Seneschal. The main butler or steward.

Serpent. I know what you're thinking. "Gee, how stupid does he think we are?" But seriously: go back and look a few pages into Chapter Three of *The Silver Chair*. This ain't a snake we're talking about here. The serpent was an odd wind instrument built during the Seventeenth and Eighteenth Centuries, and shaped in serpentine form. It had six finger-holes, requiring both hands to play. Which made it pretty difficult to hold, too—just like a serpent!

Sharp's the Word. An admonishment to be alert. In origin, used to alert shopkeepers to the threat of shoplifting.

Sherbet. Not the frozen, ice cream-like dessert we know now. This is taken from the Turkish word, meaning a sometimes snow-cooled fruit drink.

Siccus. An ancient and learned medical doctor.

Silenus. A satyr of Greek mythology, one with a fondness for wine. Satyrs were similar in appearance to fauns, like Tumnus, but apparently with fewer humanoid features.

Skirling. Shrill. A skirl is the sound made by Scottish bagpipes.

Sledge. Sometimes synonymous with "sled," but indicating one of heavy construction and pulled by animals. (A sleigh is a lighter form of sledge.)

Snipe. A type of bird, which really does exist. Whatever you do, though, NEVER go on a snipe hunt if someone asks you to. Trust me.

Stag. Not an old bachelor, such as C. S. Lewis himself and his brother Warnie were, but an adult male deer.

Stern. This is used as a noun here, not an adjective, so there's no missing word. The stern is the rear portion of a ship (synonymous, more or less, with "aft" or sometimes "poop," as in "the poop deck"—and I actually think Lewis uses this latter term far more frequently in this book than is proper for an adult).

Stiff. Since locks are generally made of iron or steel, yes—most locks are indeed stiff. What Lewis means, though, is that the lock was slightly rusty, making it hard to turn the key.

Strain. A bit of the melody of a song.

Strait Promise. A forced oath obtained from the loser in a battle.

Sucks. Wow. I was kind of surprised to see Lewis use this expression. I really don't know how he intended it. Possibly, this is a shortened version of the aphorism about teaching your grandmother to suck eggs, which would make it an expression conveying uselessness.

Suit. Courtship. Edmund was suggesting to Rabadash that his pursuit of Susan may be coming up short.

Tash. This name for the "false god" of the Calormenes is apparently derived from one of the names of Ahura Mazda, the god of Zoroastrianism. Ahura Mazda is sometimes called Tasho or Tashea, the Designer.

Teetotaller. One who, like my parents (but not me), abstains completely from the consumption of alcoholic beverages of any type. The term apparently originated with the British "temperance" movement. (And that's another definition we won't get into here.)

Term-time. In American schools, we usually refer to "semesters," "trimesters" or "quarters." In college, though, we still refer at times to "term papers," but usually the word "term" is reserved for a prison sentence. For the Pevensie kids, this just meant it was time to go back to school.

Tilt. The act of jousting.

Tongues. This is food. Really. At one time, the tongues of various animals (usually cattle or game) were considered delicacies. Today, you can still get tongue from your butcher, but you don't typically see tongue served with your fries at Mickey D's.

Touch One's Cap. Give deference to. It used to be the custom, when passing a respectable person, to touch one's hand to the brim of one's cap and bow ever so slightly.

Turkish Delight. A cube-shaped jelly-like candy. Think of sticky Gummi Bears covered in powdered sugar. Sort of.

Undressed. Not naked, but untreated. Bandages are used to "dress wounds."

Wallet. Not the thing you stick in your back pocket. Heavens, no. Caspian's pockets couldn't have been that big. No. A wallet of this sort is a knapsack (or backpack, if you don't know what a knapsack is).

Warped In. Towed in by a line.

Wars of the Roses. Not a reference to that movie starring Michael Douglas, just so we're clear. This is a reference to violent struggles over the succession to the British throne.

Water-butt. A portable water container. Think of a Gatorade barrel, only made out of wood.

Wheedling. The art of flattery, of getting what one wants through manipulation.

White Feather. A sign of cowardice. During World War I in Britain, white feathers were given to young men who had not joined the army. It was intended as an insulting gesture.

White Stag. From Celtic mythology, a sign that the end is near.

Wigwam. I grew up thinking this was the same thing as a tepee. But it's not. The tepee was used by the Plains Indians, while the wigwam (or wickiup) was a bark- and skin-covered dwelling used by Indians on the Eastern seaboard of America. The wigwam's framework is shaped kind of like a beehive. So what's a Marsh-wiggle doing in a wigwam? And how on earth does Lewis know anything about wigwams? Well, he knows about that serpent instrument, so I guess he knows everything.

Wire. A telegram. Before the telegraph, messages were delivered by hand. With the advent of the telegraph, messages could be sent electronically, "by wire." A message sent "by wire" came to be known as "a wire."

Wireless. A radio. It's unusual for an adjective to be used as a noun, but unusual devices sometimes acquire unusual names. In the first part of the twentieth century, the idea of receiving voices through the air (that is, via wireless technology) was as novel as cell phones are today.

Wood Sorel. Oxalis, a wild herb.

Wooses. Possibly related to Tolkien's "woses," or wild primitive woodmen.

World Ash Tree. Yggdrasil, the tree of life (so to speak) from Norse mythology; as documented in the Younger Edda.

Yard. The cross-piece on the mast, from which a square sail would be hung.

Yeomanry. Historically, the yeomanry were neither serfs nor nobles, but free craftsmen, cotters, soldiers, etc. In Medieval times, they represented a large middle class already accustomed to self discipline in small businesses and trades. The class included blacksmiths, archers, shoemakers, chandlers, etc. Later, "the Yeomanry" became the title of one branch of the British military.

Works Cited

Chesterton, G. K. *The Defendant*. London: J. M. Dent, 1901.

Hooper, Walter. *C. S. Lewis: A Companion and Guide*. New York: Harper, 1996.

Lewis, C. S. *The Four Loves*. New York: Harcourt Brace Jovanovich, 1960.

---. *God in the Dock*. Ed. Walter Hooper. Grand Rapids: Eerdmans, 1970.

---. *The Great Divorce*. New York: Macmillan, 1946.

---. *The Horse and His Boy*. New York: Scholastic Inc., 1988.

---. *The Last Battle*. New York: Scholastic Inc., 1988.

---. *Letters to Malcolm: Chiefly on Prayer*. New York: Harcourt Brace Jovanovich, 1964.

---. *The Lion, the Witch and the Wardrobe*. New York: Scholastic Inc., 1988.

---. *The Magician's Nephew*. New York: Scholastic Inc., 1988.

---. *Mere Christianity*. New York: Macmillan, 1960.

---. *Of Other Worlds: Essays and Stories*. New York: Harcourt Brace Jovanovich, First Harvest edition, 1975.

---. *Perelandra*. New York: Collier Books, First Paperback Edition, 1965.

---. *The Problem of Pain*. New York: Macmillan, 1962.

---. *Prince Caspian*. New York: Scholastic Inc., 1988.

---. *The Silver Chair*. New York: Scholastic Inc., 1988.

---. *Surprised by Joy*. New York: Harcourt Brace Jovanovich, 1984.

---. *The Voyage of the* Dawn Treader. New York: Scholastic Inc., 1988.

Martindale, Wayne. *Beyond the Shadowlands: C. S. Lewis on Heaven and Hell*. Wheaton: Crossway Books, 2005.

Tolkien: A Celebration. Joseph Pearce, ed. London: Fount, 1999.

Tolkien, J. R. R. *The Tolkien Reader*. New York: Ballantine Books, 1966.

Kathy Bledsoe

Is a writer with a degree in Theology from Puget Sound Christian College in Everett, Washington. She teaches adults at Highline Christian Church and is also an office administrator for the Highline School District.

George Rosok

Has a B.A. in Journalism from the University of Montana. He is active in community theatre and is a manager in the telecommunications industry.

Greg Wright

Is Writer in Residence at Puget Sound Christian College in Everett, Washington. Greg is the author of Peter Jackson in Perspective: The Power Behind Cinema's The Lord of the Rings *(Hollywood Jesus Books, 2004), as well as* Tolkien in Perspective: Sifting the Gold from the Glitter *(VMI, 2003).*

Wright, Jenn

Is an editor and writer with degrees in Literature and Theology. She was a regular columnist for the online journal After Eden *(www.hollywoodjesus.com/after_eden.htm) until it ceased publication in 2005. In her spare time, she is Lead Unit Secretary at Regional Hospital in Tukwila, Washington.*

Printed in the United States
37222LVS00002B/532-627

9 780975 957752